"This is an engaging, light-hearted t
defense of Lewis's *Narnia*, and of th
ment. Taliaferro makes good sense of the theological notion that
Christ 'paid the price of sin' and of the moral consistency of Aslan's
'ransom' and rescue of the young Edmund, answering objections
to both with sympathy and precision. A book that literary critics
and Christian theologians alike should learn from."
—**Stephen R. L. Clark**
University of Liverpool

"Taliaferro brings to this project warm affection for Lewis and his
Chronicles as well as critical expertise. He deftly plumbs the depths
of these delightful stories to give us a creative version of the ran-
som theory of atonement that skillfully avoids its famous flaws.
This is Narnian theology at its sparkling best!"
—**Jerry Walls**
Houston Baptist University

"This book is a delight to read. Like Lewis himself, Taliaferro
combines imagination, erudition, and philosophical acumen with
a refreshing clarity of expression. Taliaferro's playfulness and gen-
erosity of spirit shine through his prose, allowing his insights to
be easily shared by the reader. One's views of both atonement and
Narnia will be the better for having read this fine book."
—**Victoria S. Harrison**
University of Macau

"Charles Taliaferro is well known for handling heavy topics with a
light touch. In this illuminating book he explores one of the knotti-
est problems in Christian doctrine by drawing on both philosophy
and fairytales to enhance our understanding of the atonement.
The enthusiasm and joy which he brings to this task is infectious."
—**Robert MacSwain**
The University of the South

"Charles Taliaferro is one of the most creative philosophers I know. His *A Narnian Vision of Christian Atonement* combines incisive theological knowledge with deep religious sensitivity, written in his characteristic entertaining style. Taliaferro shows us how theology can be fun."

—Linda Zagzebski
University of Oklahoma, emerita

"Charles Taliaferro offers a deep, challenging, and insightful presentation of a ransom theory of atonement. With surprising brevity, *A Narnian Vision of Atonement* manages not only to cast light on the writings of C. S. Lewis, but also to engage with ancient and modern philosophy, Christian scriptures and theology, and even Shakespeare. Like the theory it espouses, this book could help liberate persons from prisons of our own making."

—Matthew Dickerson
Co-author of *Narnia and the Fields of Arbol*

"In this fun and fascinating book, Professor Taliaferro wonderfully illustrates how C. S. Lewis's *Chronicles of Narnia* can provide us with a fresh, youthful vision of a profound, ancient theological view. Even readers who are unconvinced by the ransom theory Taliaferro defends will be inspired and intrigued by his invitation to see, through imaginative eyes, the incredible beauty and immense costliness of the atoning work of Christ."

— Adam C. Pelser
United States Air Force Academy

"Taliaferro skillfully applies his keen philosophical mind to Lewis's imaginative reasoning about theology. The result is a powerfully suggestive rehabilitation of the Ransom Theory, lately an oft-maligned theory of atonement. *A Narnian Vision of the Atonement* provocatively—even magically—demonstrates the genius of Lewis and his relevance for theology and life. Taliaferro's book is philosophical theology at its best: full of wonder; rigorous, clear, and faithful to Scripture; historically informed; and just plain fun."

—Paul M. Gould
Palm Beach Atlantic University

A Narnian Vision of the Atonement

A Narnian Vision *of the* Atonement

A Defense of the Ransom Theory

CHARLES TALIAFERRO

CASCADE *Books* · Eugene, Oregon

A NARNIAN VISION OF THE ATONEMENT
A Defense of the Ransom Theory

Cascade Books
An Imprint of Wipf and Stock Publishers
199 W. 8th Ave., Suite 3
Eugene, OR 97401

www.wipfandstock.com

PAPERBACK ISBN: 978-1-6667-9654-4
HARDCOVER ISBN: 978-1-6667-9653-7
EBOOK ISBN: 978-1-6667-9652-0

Cataloguing-in-Publication data:

Names: Taliaferro, Charles [author].

Title: A Narnian vision of the atonement : a defense of the ransom theory / Charles Taliaferro.

Description: Eugene, OR: Cascade Books, 2022 | Includes bibliographical references.

Identifiers: isbn 978-1-6667-9654-4 (paperback) | isbn 978-1-6667-9653-7 (hardcover) | isbn 978-1-6667-9652-0 (ebook)

Subjects: LCSH: Lewis, C. S. (Clive Staples), 1898-1963—Religion | Lewis, C. S. (Clive Staples), 1898-1963—Lion, the witch, and the wardrobe | Lewis, C. S. (Clive Staples), 1898-1963—Chronicles of Narnia | Narnia (Imaginary place) | Atonement | Redemption | Salvation

Classification: PR6023.E926 T35 2022 (print) | PR6023.E926 (ebook)

VERSION NUMBER 081222

For Dr. Paul Reasoner, who often reminds me of the Professor in *The Lion, the Witch and the Wardrobe.*

For the Reverend Lisa Wiens Heinsohn, rector of St. John's Episcopal Church in Minneapolis, with gratitude for her leadership, sage and brave.

"The lion has roared,
who will not fear?
The LORD God has spoken,
who can but prophesy?"

—Amos 3:8

"And throughout all Eternity
I forgive you, you forgive me.
As our dear Redeemer said:
'This the Wine, and this the Bread.'"

—William Blake, "Broken Love"

"One day, you will be old enough
to start reading fairytales again."

—C. S. Lewis's dedication of *The Lion, the Witch
and the Wardrobe* to his Godchild Lucy Barfield

Contents

Acknowledgements

To properly acknowledge my gratitude requires three brief sketches.

I first read C. S. Lewis's *The Chronicles of Narnia* in 1972 as a nineteen-year-old in the English L'Abri, a vibrant Christian community southwest of London, where I was recovering from a couple of dodgy years in the United States counter-culture. Perhaps that community was the perfect shelter ("L'Abri" is French for "shelter") to enter Narnia, as members of the community live, work, and study in a grand Manor House, not unlike the Professor's large country home in *The Lion, the Witch and the Wardrobe*.[1] I am deeply thankful for the work of Ranald Macaulay, the director of the community at the time.

Second, after nine years in graduate school and five years teaching, I presented a Narnian theory of the atonement in 1986 to a group of sleepy philosophers on a warm, summer afternoon near the end of a two-month philosophy workshop in the Pacific Northwest of the United States. In essence, I defended the atonement narrative in *The Lion, the Witch and the Wardrobe*, and then used that defense to articulate and defend what is called *the ransom theory* in Christian theology. I wish I could report that everyone broke into jovial cheering and Aslan himself came roaring

---

1. The story of my recovery from psychotropic drugs and secular existentialism is recounted in my book *Love. Love. Love: Light Reflections on Love, Life, and Death*, see the chapter "Drugs, a Bear, and an Owl: A Testimony." The title of the book comes from my father's words to me before he died in 2004. Holding my hand, he repeated the word "love" three times.

into our packed, somewhat gloomy seminar room. While it was quite clear that did *not* happen (the younger professors were not impressed that I used a fairytale to practice philosophy), thank heavens there was one senior philosopher present, Richard Purtill of Western Washington University, who wrote about Lewis and authored fantasy books of his own as well as an authoritative textbook on logic. Purtill enthusiastically announced that my proposal to use *The Chronicles of Narnia* philosophically was a good reason why we should have the workshop at all. Purtill contended that Lewis's talent for good fiction and fairytales was what made him so talented in philosophical work.[2] I am certain that this was a minority view at the time (and, incidentally, Purtill never told me whether he accepted my Narnian theory of the atonement), but at a time when I felt like crawling under a rock, his support meant the world to me. I gratefully acknowledge my debt to Richard Purtill (1931–2016) and his inspiring devotion to logic as well as the imagination. Encouraged by Purtill to not stick to conventional academics, I went on to publish "A Narnian Theory of the Atonement" in *The Scottish Journal of Theology* in 1998, which led to my giving an invited presentation on the atonement in Narnia at the Oxford C. S. Lewis Society in 1992, and then in 2005 to co-author with Rachel Traughber (a gifted St. Olaf philosophy and music major) a defense of the exchange between Aslan and the Witch in *The Chronicles of Narnia and Philosophy: The Lion, The Witch, and The Worldview.*[3]

Third, I confess that the occasion for beginning this book is quite eccentric. My thoughts turned to writing about Narnia again when I recently became astonished by just how much the image or symbol of a lion has been with me for decades: a lion is part of the crest of St. Olaf College where I have taught for thirty-six years (a lion is also the school mascot and the college motto that I

2. Many years later, Purtill put this point in print in his entry "C. S. Lewis" in the prestigious *Encyclopedia of Philosophy*: "The talent that made him a good writer of fiction carries over to his nonfictional work; he is an artist, as well as a logician, and employs a gift for metaphor and analogy in his statements of arguments" (p. 310). The same may be said about Purtill.

3. Taliaferro and Traughber, "The Atonement in Narnia."

usually wear features about thirty lions), the lion is the symbol of St. Mark's Cathedral, which I attend periodically (the lion being the symbol of St. Mark), a lion is the symbol of the city of Venice, where I have done substantial research, and recently I have been made a member of a center at Cambridge University, whose crest includes four lions. No doubt all a coincidence, but when I received a request in the fall of 2021 for a copy of my first Narnian article from a philosophy professor at the U.S. Air Force Academy (the Air Force participates in African Lion 2021, the largest multinational operation including NATO to protect Northern Africa), I thought that *maybe* the last line in the 2008 Narnian film, *Prince Caspian*, directed by Andrew Adamson, from a song titled "The Call," spoke to me. As Lucy (played brilliantly by Sophie Wilcox) reluctantly takes leave of Aslan (Liam Neeson's provides Aslan's voice) and returns from Narnia to The Strand in the London Underground, surrounded by people in military uniforms and young people in school outfits, Regina Spektor sings about returning and not having to say goodbye.[4]

No. I am *not* claiming that Aslan himself has called me to write this book for fans of Narnia and an Air Force professor! In these Acknowledgements I am simply trying to acknowledge, undoubtedly in a clumsy way, how I first came to the topic of Narnia and the atonement, how grateful I am to Purtill as a philosophical role model to persevere in using a fairytale to practice philosophy, and how years later an uncanny barrage of lion images plus a request from the Air Force prompted me *not* to say goodbye to *The Chronicles of Narnia*. Instead, this cascade of events led me to revisit the *Chronicles* in a renewed quest to discover what we might learn from Aslan and the other characters in Narnia: about ourselves, philosophy, and theology.

Above all, I am deeply grateful for the support and work of Revd. Dr. Robin Parry of Cascade Books. I am also very grateful for comments on early versions of this manuscript from Kirk Allison, Matthew Dickerson, Tom Erickson, Karen Evans, Stewart

4. Regina Spektor, "The Call." Lyrics © 2008 Soviet Kitsch Music, Wonderland Music Co. Inc., Wonderland Music Company Inc.

Goetz, Adam Johnson, Edward Langerak, Barclay Marcell, Alyssa Medin, David O'Hara, Adam Pelsner, Christophe Porot ("Coach"), Michael Peterson, and Father Marcus Vanderhill.

Introduction

Imagine that there is more to reality than the mundane world we inhabit. Imagine that just beyond our sight and touch and hearing lies another world, one populated by fantastic creatures, great and small—dragons, centaurs, unicorns, dwarves, tree spirits, and talking beavers, to mention just a few. Imagine too that this world is a conflict zone between the forces of good and evil, epitomized most dramatically in the figures of Aslan, the great Lion, and Jadis, the powerful and twisted witch. What if you could pass between our own world and this enchanting and terrifying reality? What an adventure that would be! Such is the invitation offered to readers in *The Chronicles of Narnia*, a series of seven books, written over seven years by C. S. Lewis (1898–1963).

Clive Staples Lewis was a scholar of medieval and Renaissance literature at Oxford and Cambridge universities. He was known as "Jack" among family and friends and was a prolific writer, not only of academic works but also of immensely popular books in multiple genres, including fairytales (such as the Narnia books), supernatural narratives, poetry, science fiction, a novel (in which he re-tells the classical myth of Cupid and Psyche), short stories, and multiple essays and books.

Lewis is well known for imaginatively engaging and presenting Christian faith for a wide array of readers in ways that are accessible, robust, witty, and not weighed down with jargon. His focus was on communicating and defending what he called "mere Christianity"—the common, orthodox faith shared by all the branches of the church. Although himself an Anglican he was not invested in defending tradition-specific forms of the faith, such as Catholicism or Anglicanism. Rather, it was the *common core* at the heart of all the traditional churches that inspired and motivated him.

C. S. Lewis famously entered popular culture when he made the cover of *Time* on September 7, 1947, on the occasion of the publication of his *Screwtape Letters*, a sardonic correspondence between an old devil and a young one. Lewis appears on the cover of the magazine with a devil, complete with a pitchfork, by his left shoulder. Today, he is celebrated in the context of Lewis societies, institutes, workshops, conferences, and chat forums, some of which are dedicated to Narnia. Among all his works, *The Chronicles of Narnia* has proved to be especially enduring. Over 100 million copies have been sold, in forty-seven translations, and it has also been adapted for film, television, theatre, and radio. These stories of the world through the wardrobe will doubtlessly continue to fuel the imaginations of children and adults alike for a long time to come.

Having begun this introduction by paying homage to Lewis, it needs to be noted upfront that this book is not first and foremost about Lewis. There are abundant books about Lewis, including a very short one that I wrote ages ago on Lewis' spirituality, *Praying with C. S. Lewis: Companions for the Journey*.[1] Instead, this book is about a creation of Lewis': Narnia and Christian accounts of atonement (literally, at-one-ment) between God and humans. I recount many Narnian narratives, especially in the first and last chapters of this book, so that it is not *absolutely essential* that you have read

---

1. I have also contributed to Werther and Werther, eds., *C. S. Lewis's List: The Top Ten Books That Influenced Him*, and MacSwain and Ward, eds., *The Cambridge Companion to C. S. Lewis*. There are at least thirty books I would like to recommend here on Lewis, but space allows me to single out only six: the unsurpassed encyclopedic work *C. S. Lewis: A Companion & Guide* by Walter Hooper (1931–2020), who dedicated his life to promoting work by Lewis; there are two outstanding books by Stewart Goetz that I highly recommend: *C. S. Lewis* and *A Walking Tour with C. S. Lewis*; see also Peterson, *C. S. Lewis and the Christian Worldview*; Purtill, *C. S. Lewis and the Case for Christianity*; Dickerson and O'Hara, *Narnia and the Fields of Arbol*.

the *Chronicles* recently (or have read them at all) to understand the philosophical theology that follows, but if you have not read them, I recommend dropping everything and doing a deep dive into these spellbinding books. They are fairytales that can be appreciated by readers of any age.

Notwithstanding some philosophical grownups who disparage fairytales, Lewis and his friend J. R. R. Tolkien, certainly a mastermind of high fantasy, contended that fairytales can convey truths to readers who might otherwise resist them if presented in a conventional format. They can open us up to new ways of seeing and experiencing life that help us to escape the entrapping assumptions of our surrounding culture. Indeed, Tolkien championed the idea that fairytales are escapist, commenting that the people who frown on escapist literature are like jailers. Both Tolkien and Lewis lamented that we live in a mechanical age that makes us think that industry and robots are the most evident, inescapable realities. In his famous essay "On Fairy Stories," Tolkien strikes back: "The notion that motor-cars are more 'alive' than, say, centaurs or dragons is curious; that they are more 'real' than, say, horses is pathetically absurd. How real, how startlingly alive is a factory chimney compared with an elm-tree?"[2] Both Tolkien and Lewis used fantastic literature to display an alternative world shimmering with heroic love. Moreover, fairytales can speak to the longing we have as children or at any age for an enchanted fulfillment beyond the ordinary. Lewis defended fairytales as arousing the imagination of children and others to open us up to an enriching enchantment:

> Does anyone suppose that he [a lover of fairytales] really and prosaically longs for all of the dangers and discomforts of a fairytale, really wants dragons in contemporary England? It would be much truer to say that fairy land arouses a longing for he knows not what. It stirs and troubles him (to his life-long enrichment) with the dim sense of something beyond his reach and, far from dulling or emptying the actual world, gives it a new

2. See: https://coolcalvary.files.wordpress.com/2018/10/on-fairy-stories1.pdf. For a brilliant philosophical use of fairytales, see Harper, *Sleeping Beauty and Other Essays*.

dimension of depth. He does not despise real woods because he has read of enchanted woods: the reading makes all real woods a little enchanted.[3]

In this book, I focus on what we may learn from the narratives of the *Chronicles* rather than engage in literary analysis, but I occasionally point out how the books relate to traditional fairytales.

Fans differ in terms of the best order to read the *Chronicles* today. In 2001 HarperCollins, published in a single volume the books in the sequence of (as it were) Narnian time, beginning with the creation of Narnia (*The Magician's Nephew*) and ending with the ending or transfiguration of Narnia (*The Last Battle*).[4] I will use the HarperCollins text for page numbers in what follows, as it is readily available to readers. But the books were written and published beginning with a tale in the middle of Narnian history, *The Lion, the Witch and the Wardrobe*. Although I have no objection to reading the *Chronicles* in the HarperCollins sequence, there are two reasons why I personally recommend reading the *Chronicles* in the order of publication.

First, we have reason to believe that Lewis began the *Chronicles* without having planned out any of the future books. Beginning to read what Lewis began writing can give one a sense of how the *Chronicles* evolved in Lewis' imagination. I am continually amazed in my re-reading of how the story of what might have been a single, stand-alone book grew into a series of seven.

Second, it is true that, from a Narnian perspective *The Lion, the Witch and the Wardrobe*, begins in the middle of things (*in medias res*), but, after all, isn't that what it is like for us? From the perspective of the world we live in, we were each of us born in "the middle of things" and will (probably), unless there is a huge apocalypse, die in what is in the middle of things (many of our relations, students,

---

3. Lewis cited by Walter Hooper in *C. S. Lewis: A Companion & Guide*, 399.

4. There is some reason to believe that Lewis himself preferred that the *Chronicles* be read in terms of Narnian chronology, beginning with *The Magician's Nephew*; see Schultz and West, eds., *The C. S. Lewis Readers' Encyclopedia*, 121.

colleagues, and so on, will live on). For this reason, I enjoy reading the books in a way that we ourselves approach life: we don't begin life with a God's-eye point of view, but find ourselves in the world, helter-skelter, and only gradually sort out a bigger picture. That is why I enjoy re-reading the *Chronicles* beginning with *The Lion, the Witch and the Wardrobe*, and then gradually moving back in Narnian time to the creation of Narnia and, eventually, reaching the epic climax at the end of the *Chronicles* with *The Last Battle*.[5]

Here are the book titles, the dates published, and a list of the abbreviations I use in this book.

- 1950. *The Lion, the Witch and the Wardrobe*. (Abbreviated as *Lion*.)

- 1951. *Prince Caspian*. (Abbreviated as *Caspian*.)

- 1952. *The Voyage of the Dawn Treader*. (Abbreviated as *Voyage*.)

- 1953. *The Silver Chair*. (Abbreviated as *Chair*.)

- 1954. *The Horse and His Boy*. (Abbreviated as *Horse*.)

- 1955. *The Magician's Nephew*. (Abbreviated as *Magician*.)

- 1956. *The Last Battle*. (Abbreviated as *Battle*.)

Each of these books are expertly illustrated by Pauline Baynes, whose drawings appear in some of J. R. R. Tolkien's shorter books, such as the playful, lyrical poem *The Adventures of Tom Bombadil*. HarperCollins has reproduced Baynes' winsome illustrations in

---

5. The suggestion that we read the *Chronicles* in the order of publication is supported by Peter Schakel: "The only reason to read *The Magician's Nephew* first . . . is for the chronological order of events, and that, as every storyteller knows, is quite unimportant as a reason. Often the early events in a sequence have a greater impact or effect as a flashback, told after later events which provide background and establish perspective. So it is . . . with the Chronicles. The artistry, the archetypes, and the pattern of Christian thought all make it preferable to read the books in the order of their publication." *The C. S. Lewis's Readers' Encyclopedia*, 121–22. If you read the books in the order they were published, you will come to enjoy later in the series (in *Magician*) the backstory concerning the Lion, the Witch, the wardrobe, the Professor, and the lamppost.

their published *Chronicles*. While I do not address the illustrations in this book, I recommend spending time with them in your reading, as they enhance the stories.[6]

Most of the attention at the outset of this book will be given to *Lion*, but I address the other six volumes as well. Chapter five takes up several important elements about their mature insights on themes such as faith, wagering on what is true, and magic. On the latter, some Christians find magic a problem. In the second century *Didache*, there is this simple injunction: "You shall not practice magic."[7] In light of such dictums, what should we make of all the magic in the *Chronicles*?

On the atonement: virtually all Christians believe that Jesus Christ plays a vital role in the atonement between God and us. While there are abundant biblical passages to the effect that Jesus saves us from sin, death, and the power of evil, these texts are open to various accounts of just *how* Jesus' work of salvation takes place. For example, did Jesus engage in vicarious suffering in which he bore our sins or the penalty for sin? Or does Jesus save by being a supreme, spiritual exemplar, the incarnate witness to the God of love? One of the earliest accounts of Jesus' saving work has come to be referred to as *the ransom theory*. The term "ransom" occurs thirty-two times in the Bible. In Mark 10:45, for example, Jesus says "For the Son of Man"—a title that is used to refer to Jesus eighty-one times in the four Gospels—"came not to be served, but to serve, and to give his life as a *ransom* for many." Some early Christians, including Basil the Great, Gregory of Nyssa, and Origen of Alexandria, proposed that when we sin, we become captives or prisoners of Satan. In one, common version of the theory, we become liberated because Christ is a ransom paid

---

6. Lacking any artistic talent has not prevented me from sketching these drawings, a practice that I recommend as a way to study her artwork and engage Lewis' narrative visually. The HarperCollins version includes Baynes's drawing of Peter and Susan talking with the Professor, apparently substituting it for the illustration I particularly love in the Macmillan 1961 publication of *Lion* showing the Professor, Peter, and Susan looking at the country house from a distance (p. 41).

7. *Didache* 2.

to overcome Satan, sin, and death. When Satan kills Christ and Christ dies, Christ then overcomes Satan and liberates us through his resurrection. Some version of the ransom theory is in play in the *Chronicles* in which Aslan (a Christ figure) presents himself to the White Witch (a satanic figure) in exchange for securing Edmund's freedom from the Witch. Aslan is killed in Edmund's place but then rises from the dead and defeats the Witch and her army in a momentous battle.

I propose that the ransom theory is well overdue for a revival today. We need it, I maintain, because of its relevance for a matter that has received growing attention from many of us, namely, the ways we can be entrapped by past evils (such as systemic racism and sexism, and colonialism) and the need for us to be liberated from such captivity and seek restorative justice. At the heart of the ransom theory is God's act to liberate us from evil (past and present) and restore life and healing to those who have been harmed or destroyed. An advocate of a version of the ransom theory in the fourth century, Gregory Nazianzen, succinctly highlights the restorative, atoning work of Christ: "He was nailed to the wood and lifted up, but he restores us by the tree of life. . . . He dies, but he brings to life, and by his own death destroys death. He is buried, but he rises again. He descends into hell, but rescues the souls imprisoned there."[8]

However, despite its appeal to liberation and restoration, most theologians reject the ransom theory, sometimes with derision. I have a friend who, when asked if she wants wine, says "ABC" (her abbreviation for *anything but Chardonnay*); theologians today, when asked for a theory of the atonement, might well reply AVERT (meaning, *any version except ransom theory!*).

The ransom theory is rejected by many if not most Christian philosophers and theologians, both historically and today, on several grounds. Probably the most forceful objection rests on the role of Satan. In a recent, outstanding book, *A History of Western Philosophy*, C. Stephen Evans takes note of the different images of the atonement in the New Testament, acknowledging the ransom

---

8. Gregory of Nazianzen, *Third Theological Oration*, 43.

theory among early Christians as well as in C. S. Lewis' *The Lion, the Witch and the Wardrobe.* He spells out why the ransom theory is problematic both historically in our world as well as in Narnia. Because of the importance of Evans' link between early theology and *Lion,* I cite him at length:

> The New Testament itself, in describing Christ's atonement, employs different images or metaphors. Christ's death is variously described as a sacrifice, a punishment that Christ bore on behalf of humans, and as a "ransom for many." Early Christian thinker mainly relied on the last of these images, seeing Christ's death as a ransom paid by God that liberated humans from the power of sin, death, and Satan. The idea that Christ's death was a ransom is still defended, but Anselm [of Canterbury, the great philosophical theologian, 1033–1109] found it problematic in ways that many still do. If Christ's death is a ransom, to whom is the ransom paid? One might think that the answer is God, but why should God require such a ransom, and if he does, how can he pay it to himself? Many of the patristic thinkers thought that the ransom was paid to Satan. God gave his Son to Satan as a ransom for humans who were in Satan's power, but Satan did not realize that Christ would rise from death and be victorious over sin. In trying to include Jesus within his domain, Satan overreached and lost his power over humans. This idea, though beautifully presented in literary form in C. S. Lewis's *The Lion, the Witch and the Wardrobe,* also seems problematic to many. Does Satan really have some kind of rightful claim on sinful humans? Some versions of the ransom seem to involve God as tricking or deceiving Satan; it is as if Jesus were bait offered to Satan, which Satan swallowed without realizing that he thereby would be "hooked." However, it seems wrong to think of God as deceiving or tricking anyone, even Satan.[9]

A defense of the ransom theory seems to face an uphill battle, for even if one can make sense of Satan having a rightful claim over sinful humans, Satan accepting Jesus as a ransom, *and* defend

9. Evans, *A History of Western Philosophy,* 161.

the idea that the offer of Jesus as a ransom did not involve God in wrongful deception, there is the underlying, vexing problem of positing the existence of Satan at all.

While Satan and demons appear in the New Testament (there are about eighty references to demons or bad or unclean spirits in the New Testament), none of the creeds of the Christian church (the two most well-known are the Apostles' Creed and the Nicene Creed) include attesting to the reality of Satan, demons, or the demonic. Records of the early teaching (or preaching) of the apostles do not explicitly reference Satan (e.g., Peter's proclamation in Acts 2). In the *Book of Common Prayer* (BCP), those who are to be baptized are asked (or in the case of infant baptism, the sponsors of the children are asked), "Do you renounce Satan and all the spiritual forces of wickedness that rebel against God?" but contemporary Christians probably see this renunciation as a repudiation of what may be called "evil powers" (which may include wicked institutions or social systems) rather than the renunciation of an actual, supernaturally evil, incorporeal spirit. For some, Satan may be understood as a metaphor, symbol, or a personification of evil. After all, in the BCP Catechism there are these questions and answers with no allusion to Satan:

Q. How does sin have power over us?

A. Sin has power over us because we lose our liberty when our relationship with God is distorted.

Q. What is redemption?

A. Redemption is the act of God which sets us free from the power of evil, sin, and death.

The philosopher Stephen R. L. Clark remarks that while many of us do not believe in demons and magic, we seem to accept a host of other "intangible forces": "Most educated Westerners doubt the existence of *daimones* or the power of magic (but accept the existence of intangible forces we can often put to work for us, and increasingly rely on gadgets controlled by verbal commands and ciphers)."[10] We may not have magic books, but our technology makes us look a bit like the magician Prospero and his spirit servant Ariel in Shakespeare's *The Tempest*.

Still, some surveys indicate widespread belief in demons globally; and perhaps over half of the United States population still believes in demons and ghosts.[11] And some contemporary philosophers of religion have defended the coherence of believing that there are demons and angels, arguing that it is possible that such good and evil supernatural creatures exist.[12] Stephen R. L. Clark has warned us not to be so fixated on our own biology that we rule out there being radically different living, intelligent beings in our cosmos. There may be alien forms of intelligent, sapient life radically different from us:

> It is also very likely that there are species out there beyond the Sun as sapient as we are. What we imagine about them shows much more about ourselves than about biological possibility. How probable is it that we would recognize intelligence in some utterly alien form when it takes so much effort even to acknowledge that wolves or octopuses or bees have their own lives and thoughts?[13]

Given the extraordinary cost to human lives, with perhaps as many as 50,000 innocent persons were put to death in Europe as witches or demonically possessed persons in the sixteenth and seventeenth centuries, it is understandable why there is not great enthusiasm for defending the reasonability of Satan's existence. And, following Lewis' *The Screwtape Letters*, if there is a Satan, maybe Satan himself prefers us not to believe he is real. The master demon, Screwtape, advises his mentee demon to encourage

10. Clark, *Plotinus*, 10.

11. https://today.yougov.com/topics/philosophy/articles-reports/2020/10/30/ghosts-demons-exist-poll-data. See also Shell's Sober Comeback," 54: "Hell is undergoing something of a revival in American religious thought."

12. See Guthrie, *Gods of this World*.

13. Clark, "Why We Believe in Fairies."

humans from believing that devils actually exist. After all, if there is reason to think devils exist, might there also be angels? Or a God? The master demon proposes that it is better to get humans to dismiss the existence of devils as imaginary, comic caricatures:

> The fact that "devils" are predominantly *comic* figures in the modern imagination will help you. If any faint suspicion of your existence begins to arise in his mind, suggest to him a picture of something in red tights, and persuade him that since he cannot believe in that . . . he therefore cannot believe in you.[14]

Actually, perhaps Screwtape would have been pleased that the *Time* magazine cover of Lewis pictured Satan (or a devil of some sort) as a kind of cartoon.

Be that as it may, in my defense of the ransom theory *contra mundum*, I will distinguish between imagining a crude ransom paid to a supernatural jailer (a kind of theology that negotiates with terrorists) who has a right over us versus seeing the ransom exchange in the context of Christ *liberating persons from a kind of prison of our own making—a prison of sin, death, and the demonic.* The ransom theory that will emerge (in chapter three) will be neutral on whether Satan actually exists as a supernatural, wicked agent. Perhaps Satan exists, perhaps not. Still, I will use the term "demonic" to include demons (if there are any) but principally to refer to institutions and other social structures and habits that lead persons to do extraordinary evil. What I will propose is that what the ransom theory gets right is that sinful life can be very much like a prison, like being captive to wicked powers that extend beyond our individual control. And, most importantly, we ourselves can sometimes serve as our own jailers; we can wind up willingly playing the role of both prisoner and jailer.[15] After all, in *Lion*, Edmund appears to willingly align himself with the Witch. And, in that

---

14. Hooper, *C. S. Lewis: Companion & Guide*, 271.

15. There might be a kind of cosmic version of the famous 1971 Stanford Prison Experiment! Just as the Stanford students got out of control in their role playing, perhaps sinful persons can get out of control and variously play their own prisoner and guard.

context in which sinful persons are seen to be willing prisoners, I argue that the ransom of Christ is precisely what is needed to give the captives their freedom in the course of overturning sin and death. *The ransom consists in Jesus' compelling, loving sacrifice—his bearing the violent, life-denying effects of sin—that leads to resurrection and the promise of the triumph of good over evil, life with God over death and the absence of God. The ransom is the payment or the cost of Christ's freeing us from our willful imprisonment in sin.*

In both the Narnian ransom theory and the one I defend in Christian theology, the ransom is not a payment to a supernatural jailer or terrorist who has a right over us, but *the price of our rescue from evil*. While the ransom theory defended here is neutral as to whether there actually is a Satan ("Satan" might turn out to be a metaphorical personification of evil powers), I shall argue that the ransom itself (Christ's sacrifice and resurrection) cannot be a mere metaphor for there to be atonement. Of course, the atonement in Narnia is only real in the context of a work of literature (we are not to suppose that there really is a wardrobe just outside of London that can be a portal to another world), but I contend that the *Chronicles* provide us with a great lens through which to view the actual atonement in our world, as envisaged in Christian theology.

As noted earlier, common to most ransom theories is the *restoration* of that which has been harmed, imprisoned, lost, or destroyed. The Greek term for "restore" is *apokathistemi*. One of the great defenders of a ransom theory, Origen of Alexandria, looked toward the ultimate restoration, ransomed or paid for by Jesus Christ, of all creation in an apocatastasis. In developing his rich, cosmic vision of the great end state, Origen drew on Acts 3:19–21:

> Repent therefore, and turn to God so that your sins may be wiped out, so that times of refreshing may come from the presence of the Lord, and that he may send the Messiah appointed for you, that is, Jesus, who must remain in heaven until the time of universal restoration (*apokatastasis*) that God announced long ago through his holy prophets.

While the version of the ransom theory I defend in chapter three relies hugely on the theme of restoration there are many other elements that are in play, including the transfiguration of all persons, or at least those who are receptive to divine transfiguration and welcome it.

Here is an overview of this book.

Chapter one depicts and defends the atonement in Narnia. I propose there is zero lying or deception on the part of Aslan. The only lying or deception in *Lion* is carried out by Mr. Tumnus (who almost immediately repents), Edmund (who eventually repents), and the Witch (who is unrepentant). I further propose that the Witch's right over Edmund is derived from Aslan's respecting freedom in Narnia and not from the Witch having any rightful standing as a legal or royal authority. Moreover, Edmund is not freed because of a bargain with the Witch. We learn in *Magician* that Aslan makes no bargains, that the Witch is an enemy of Narnia and Aslan, and that any "promise" with the Witch to release Edmund was not a valid promise as the Witch not only did not intend to free Edmund, her plan was to kill Edmund, his siblings, and the good creatures of Narnia. The genius of the ransom in Narnia is that it involves Aslan's costly giving himself over to the Witch to demonstrate his love and power, dying and rising from the dead, and then bringing to new life those who have been turned into stone (subject to a kind of death). As part of the atonement, Aslan enjoins Edmund and the others to participate in showing courage and other virtues in the course of defeating the Witch and her army.

While I leave it to chapter one for a full presentation of my defense of atonement in Narnia, I acknowledge here that an initial reading of *Lion* may support the view that the Witch's "right to a kill" and her having "every traitor" as a "lawful prey" rests on the will of "the Emperor-beyond-the-sea." But I argue that *this right cannot be a straightforward conferral of authority by Aslan or the Emperor because the Witch herself is a traitor.* We see in *Magician*, she tries to injure or kill Aslan. If she is a traitor, and she is appointed to kill traitors, shouldn't she execute herself? I offer an alternative account of the Witch's right in what I call a *Narnian free-will defense*, according to which Aslan gives creatures free will either to choose to follow Aslan and serve the good of Narnia or to choose to follow and serve the Witch. In this framework, any right of the Witch over Edmund rests on Edmund's freely giving himself over to the Witch's domain.[16] Aslan enters that domain, not trusting in any bargain with the Witch, but in order to overturn the Witch's power, defeat wickedness, and to make death "start working backwards."

Chapter two is named in honor of St. Gregory of Nyssa (335– c. 395), one of the Cappadocian fathers (along with Basil of Caesarea and Gregory of Nazianzus). In what I will refer to as the *Gregorian ransom theory*, God does use deception (though I suggest *hiddenness* might be a better term) in the atonement. This is sometimes referred to as the *mousetrap theory*, as Jesus was set up as bait to lure Satan out to try to destroy Jesus, but then Jesus overcomes Satan through resurrection. You can see some representation of this theology in painting. For example, in the

fifteenth-century Merode Alterpiece made by the workshop of Robert Campin, Joseph is pictured making a mousetrap in his carpenter's workshop—an allusion to Jesus' future role.[17] I should add that Gregory of Nyssa was a universalist; he believed that, ultimately, God's omnipotent, overwhelming love will redeem *all* persons, including Satan. So, the mousetrap metaphor needs to be

16. The "Narnian free-will defense" is named in honor of what is known as the free will defense introduced by Alvin Plantinga, but the two have very different roles; Plantinga is concerned with the problem of the compatibility of God and evil in general, whereas my concern is with Aslan and the Witch in Narnia.

17. This image is reproduced under Creative Commons license.

seen as *non-lethal*. (Maybe if Gregory knew of the *Chronicles*, he might have prayed that Satan become like the brave talking mouse Reepicheep!) As it happens, I am sympathetic with Gregory's view of atonement and follow him on many theological positions, but I do not think it is satisfactory in its claim that Jesus Christ gave his body and blood *to Satan*. Such a notion is entirely in conflict with the New Testament portrait that Jesus gave his body and blood *to God* (not Satan) as a sacrifice (e.g., Heb 9:14), and thus he is able to offer them to his disciples in the Eucharist (see John 6:55–59; Luke 22:20; Matt 26:28; 1 Cor 11:24–30).

It is true that Jesus gives himself over to the power of Satan (called "the ruler of this world" in John) but I believe this is best thought of as not an offering to Satan in terms of self-donation. Compare giving oneself to someone in marriage versus giving up one's life by shielding children in a school shooting and (as it were) giving a terrorist a target. In the latter case, you (as it were) paid the ultimate price to save the children but you did not pay the terrorist in a way that is analogous to a (for example) financial exchange.

The term "ransom" is derived from the Latin for "buying back," *redemptio*, which became *ransoun* in Old French and then *ransom* in English. But it can also refer in English to that which redeems, releases, or provides deliverance and is not essentially linked to the idea of paying a price to a (human or demonic) kidnapper, jailer, or hostage-taker. I propose that just as in Narnia, Edmund was the beneficiary of Aslan's life, in Christianity we are the beneficiary of Christ's body and blood, given for us and offered to us (Acts 20:28; Col 1:20; Eph 1:7; Heb 9:14, 22; 10:6–9; 1 John 1:7; Rev 1:5; 7:14; 12:11).

To summarize the plot so far: the differences between atonement in Narnia and in Gregory of Nyssa's theory is in the presence or absence of deception and in the role of Satan. For Gregory, Satan is given greater standing in the ransoming of captives. God enters into a deal with Satan. True, as acknowledged above, in Narnia Aslan does give his life over in substitution for Edmund, and therefore he does give his life to the Witch, but the freeing of Edmund is not due to a bargain or to the Witch's power or due to her renunciation of Edmund. As I shall argue in chapter two, Aslan's giving his life to the Witch is more like (to use a benign example) you giving your life to a surgeon for a great purpose (it is a means to an end) than it is like giving your life to someone else, as in a wedding (which is not a means to an end but an end in itself). More on this later!

In chapter three, The Christus Victor ransom theory is advanced and defended. It has more in keeping with atonement in Narnia than the Gregorian theory. It involves no wrongful deception by God and sees the redeeming gift of God's body and blood as that which is given, not as a payment to Satan, but for the transfiguration of wrongdoers. In their transfiguration, persons come to have a new identity oriented toward God's truth, goodness, and beauty. According to this ransom theory, atonement involves five stages:

1. sorrowful confession,

2. repentance and double-movement,

3. forgiveness,

4. care and coordination, and

5. transfiguration through restitution.

In this account, God through Christ is victorious over sin, death, and the demonic, where term "demonic" refers demons (if there are any) and to those factors that ensnare or trap us in evil, whether they be institutions, social conditions, the unrepented for and unhealed past, or anything else.

At its heart, then, the Christus Victor ransom theory claims that God defeats sin, death, and the demonic by Christ's birth, teaching, miracles, and Christ enduring the effects of sin, actual death, and all suffering inflicted by demonic powers. Christ redeems or frees us as we undertake five stages in response to Christ's powerful, irresistible, resurrected life. In a nutshell, the spirit of this ransom theory is reflected in the Paschal Troparion, an Easter proclamation:

Christ is risen from the dead,
Trampling down death by death,
And on those in the tombs
Bestowing life.

The themes of transfiguration and restitution are pivotal in this triumph of life. Transfiguration is important rather than what may be called *bare restitution*. To use a ghastly example, if I have done some grave wrong—such as committing homicide—God's bringing the person back to life will not be redemptive at all if I set out to kill the person again! In the Christus Victor model, the restoration of what has been lost needs to be seen as part of wrongdoers repenting and participating in this redeeming restoration. I suggest that part of the New Testament teachings on Jesus giving us his body and blood is about our being incorporated into a transformed identity with Jesus and a participation in the life of God.

Chapter four is intended to be a *friendly chapter*. Multiple theories of atonement have been advanced to avoid the ransom theory at any cost. There are various accounts attributed to Anselm that involve the satisfaction of God's justice, there are penal substitution accounts involving vicarious suffering, there are exemplar models, and recent accounts by Philip Quinn, Richard Purtill, Richard Swinburne, and Eleonore Stump. In this chapter *I do not criticize these theories,* but I argue that they might each have more force if they are paired with the Christus Victor ransom theory. I hope that this chapter might turn the *anything but the ransom theory* theologians around!

The title of chapter five, "Redeeming Narnia," may seem ironic. In this introduction and the four chapters that follow I draw on the *Chronicles* to offer what I believe to be a defensible account of redemption in Christian theology; why, then, think the *Chronicles of Narnia* themselves require redemption? There is some rueful, personal background to this chapter. After my presentation on the atonement in Narnia at a meeting of the Oxford C. S. Lewis Society in 1992, there was the following, memorable objection from a British scholar: Even if the exchange between Aslan and the Witch has integrity, "the whole framework is childish. They are, after all, *children books*" (emphasis his). I was not prepared for this broad-side at a meeting where I was expecting die-hard Narnia fans. (I am withholding the name of the fellow as I did not get permission to identify him.) My critic did not object to fairytales *per se*, nor did he object to Lewis' Christian faith nor to Lewis' treatment of the character Susan (because this is an objection that is so wide-spread recently, I address it at the end of chapter one). He instead objected that all the magic, the reckless disregard for a reasonable bridge between Narnia and our world, plus some lurking cultural prejudice, make the *Chronicles* (in his words, as I recall them) "a platform that is too airy-fairy to launch serious theology." Perhaps this critic is an outlier in the present context; after all, I have writ-ten this book largely for those who, like me, love what we take to be Lewis' brilliant vision of Narnia. And yet, if this book truly is an *affaire d'amour*, then a final chapter is warranted both to respond specifically to the Oxford critic as well as to address wary readers not yet convinced that the *Chronicles* as a whole are indeed a sound launching pad for serious theology. (As it happens, Lewis might welcome the metaphor of a launching pad, given that his science fiction trilogy has a rocket launch in the first book.) Chapter five, then, is a kind of act of reciprocation; because I have used most of this book to draw on the *Chronicles* to defend a ransom theory, the least I can do at the end of this book is to show my gratitude by defending the *Chronicles* themselves in lieu of any persistent, lingering criticism.

In *Lion*, the four children enter Narnia through a wardrobe, in *Caspian* the four are magically transported to Narnia from a London tube station. . . . Less dramatically, I ask you to join me now in Narnia imaginatively simply by turning this page.

Chapter One

Atonement in Narnia

*L*ion begins during World War II when four siblings in the Pevensie family—Peter (age thirteen), Susan (twelve), Edmund (ten), and Lucy (eight)—are evacuated from London because of the air-raids. While we are not told this by Lewis, such evacuations became intensified with the systematic bombing of London by the German Luftwaffe beginning in early September 1940.

The two brothers and two sisters are welcomed by an old professor who lives in a large house in the country. As the Pevensies explore the house, Lucy lags behind her siblings and enters a large wardrobe that leads her to a snowy wood where, in the middle of a clearing by a lamppost, she meets a talking faun named Mr. Tumnus. The faun explains that Lucy has come from "the Wild Woods of the West" and is now in Narnia.[1] Lucy is addressed by Mr. Tumnus as coming from a world made up of Sons of Adam and Daughters of Eve.[2] Mr. Tumnus and Lucy seem to form a lovely bond, waking arm in arm to his home, where he makes her tea and

1. Lewis, *Chronicles*, 115. As noted in the introduction, all citations of the *Chronicles* are given by page number in the HarperCollins edition, 2001.

2. It is curious that the people of our world are not called Sons and Daughters (or descendants) of Adam and Eve. Perhaps Lewis' gendered pairing suggests that males are represented by Adam and females by Eve in the story of Eden and the fall. In any case, the first wrongdoing or sin in Narnia reverses the Edenic narrative, for it is the male, Digory, who commits the first wrong or sin in Narnia, and it is the female, Polly, who seeks to stop the male wrongdoer.

presents her with a cake, toast, and other treats while telling her about Narnia—its nymphs, dryads, dwarfs—and playing the flute.

Mr. Tumnus then breaks down crying and makes a dreadful confession: Narnia is not safe. It is under the power of the White Witch. Her control over Narnia is cruel; she demands obedience of Narnians, including Mr. Tumnus, or face torture and being turned into stone (apparently a kind of death) and she controls the seasons. The Witch has placed Narnia in a perpetual winter without Christmas—"Christmas" is not explained in terms of the feast of the incarnation but in this context might be taken to be a time of festivity with the giving and receiving of gifts. Worst of all, Mr. Tumnus tells Lucy he was a kidnapper, for he only feigned his friendly hospitality in welcoming her into his cave; his real aim was to lure Lucy to sleep so that he would turn her over to the White Witch. He is shaken with remorse, for he asks Lucy's forgiveness and offers to helps her get home. Lucy responds that she can indeed forgive him, and perhaps as a sign of this accord, they shake hands, and she tells Mr. Tumnus that it is her hope that he will not get into any trouble for her sake.

So, the first tale of betrayal in *Lion* leads to reconciliation through a sorrowful confession and Mr. Tumnus' effort to undo the damage by risking his life helping Lucy escape the Witch's capture and return home. While the wrong of Mr. Tumnus is serious, even a grave wrong (the attempted kidnapping of a child!), he appears to be unwillingly (or not happily) in the Witch's service, and the process of reconciliation (a kind of atonement) with Lucy need not require further sacrifice. However, the next betrayal in *Lion* is more sinister and virtually impossible for anyone other than Aslan to reverse and put things right.

Upon Lucy's return through the wardrobe, she tells her siblings about Narnia, but meets with immediate skepticism. They all go to the wardrobe but see it as just an ordinary wardrobe and not a portal to another world. Peter and Susan think Lucy is lying and they seek to down-play the event, while Edmund is spiteful and mocking.

A few days later, when playing hide-and-seek, Edmund goes through the wardrobe and into Narnia. He meets a powerful lady who appears to be Queen of Narnia. She prompts him to tell her about his siblings, reporting that one of his sisters had been to Narnia already and met a Faun. The Queen gives Edmund Turkish Delight, which he ravenously eats and finds himself craving when he has finished it. She promises to make Edmund a prince and then king of Narnia. But first he must bring his siblings to the Queen. She tantalizes him with the idea that he might straightaway go to reside with the Queen, but this would likely lead him to neglect his errand of bringing his siblings to her. The Queen drives a wedge between Edmund and his siblings. He is to engage in deception in order to deliver his siblings to the Queen.

Edmund is set up to be united or live with the Queen, being adopted as her son and heir. He is now primed to rupture his relationships with Peter, Susan, and Lucy, in a conspiracy with an evil power. He is flattered by the Queen's high praise of his prowess, of his possessing the skills needed to overcome any resistance to the Queen based on Lucy's friendship with Mr. Tumnus. Just as the Queen insinuates herself to Edmund, he distances himself from his siblings. Trying to keep the Queen's attention supremely on him, he tells her that his siblings are not at all special, implying that *he* is the interesting one, whereas they are comparatively insignificant.

While Edmund is still in Narnia, he encounters Lucy, who is so excited to see him (and confirm that Narnia is real) she does not notice at first Edmund's changed appearance: his face and speech is disdainful. Edmund's visage has changed. He is "already more than half on the side of the Witch."[3]

Lucy and Edmund return to our world, but Edmund pretends that he did not go to Narnia. Edmund's denial of Lucy's report is not detached and cool, but nasty and confrontational. The professor enters the picture and there is a fascinating dialogue with Peter and Susan about whom to believe: Lucy or Edmund. This exchange raises a great question about trust that I address in chapter five.

3. Lewis, *Chronicles*, 128.

Eventually, all four children enter Narnia. When Edmund tries to get his siblings to head in a certain direction, becomes apparent to everyone that Edmund lied about never having been to Narnia. Peter calls him a poisonous beast. Rather than confess his wrong, ask forgiveness, seek to undo the damage he caused, and be reconciled, Edmund seems bent on revenge. Rather than being ashamed of his deception, Edmund nurses the idea of humiliating his siblings, whom he thinks of as priggish and satisfied.

The children discover that Mr. Tumnus' home is in ruins and that there is a notice by the captain of the secret police that Mr. Tumnus has been arrested and is awaiting trial. Lucy is convinced that the so-called Queen is the horrible Witch who has all of Narnia under her spell, making it always winter. Edmund tries to sow dissension, questioning both whether they should trust fauns and think the Queen is a witch. Because in the story the so-called Queen is the Witch, I will refer to as the Witch for the of this chapter. (In a later book we learn that her name is Jadis, but let's stick with the Witch in the context of *Lion*.)

The children are led to the home of Mr. and Mrs. Beaver. They become convinced of the friendliness of the Beavers (after displaying a gift Lucy had given to Mr. Tumnus) and enjoy a hearty dinner, hearing about how the Witch is a descendent of Adam and his first wife, Lilith. She pretends that she is fully human, but she is not. It is feared that Mr. Tumnus has been taken to the Witch's house where he would be turned into stone. And the children learn from these friendly talking beasts of Aslan. Mr. Beaver explains that Aslan is the King, a mighty Lord who can overcome the Witch and save Mr. Tumnus. He tells the children, Aslan is often not seen, but there are reports that Aslan has returned to Narnia.

The children are alarmed when they realize that Edmund has gone missing. They want to search for Edmund, but Mr. Beaver responds that there is no use looking, because Edmund has committed treachery, and sided with the Witch. Mr. Beaver tells them that his betrayal is evident in Edmund's eyes; he has the appearance of one who has eaten the Witch's food and is now with her rather than with them.

Mr. Beaver is correct. Edmund goes to the Witch's Palace and discovers a ghastly scene in which animals and dwarfs and many other creatures have been turned into stone. Edmund tells the Witch about his siblings being in Narnia and the rumor that Aslan is now in Narnia. Edmund's calling her "Your Majesty" suggests his fealty to her; he is a subject addressing his ruler, the Queen.

There are various adventures that lead up to the atonement in Narnia—the Witch's spell over Narnia is weakening, the Witch sends agents to the home of the Beavers with the order to kill whomever they find; Edmund witnesses the Witch turning innocent creatures into stone; Aslan appears to Peter, and Peter slays an attacking, vicious wolf. The hint that the redemption of Edmund will not be easy, comes in this exchange:

> "Please—Aslan," said Lucy, "can anything be done to save Edmund?"
>
> "All shall be done," said Aslan. "But it may be harder than you think." And then he was silent again for some time. Up to that moment Lucy had been thinking how royal and strong and peaceful his face looked; now it suddenly came into her head that he looked sad as well.[4]

Events happen speedily. The Witch prepares Edmund to be killed on the Stone Table. She beckons all creatures in her realm to join her. Just as a knife is being sharpened for the killing, Narnian creatures swoop in to rescue Edmund. But when Edmund is reunited with his siblings and apologizes, all is not put right.

The Witch arrives in Aslan's camp and there is this exchange:

> "You have a traitor there, Aslan," said the Witch. Of course, everyone present knew that she meant Edmund. But Edmund had got past thinking about himself after all he'd been through and the talk he'd had that morning. He just went on looking at Aslan. It didn't seem to matter what the Witch said.
>
> "Well," said Aslan "His offence was not against you."
>
> "Have you forgotten the Deep Magic?" asked the Witch.

4. Lewis, *Chronicles*, 169.

"Let us say I have forgotten it," answered Aslan gravely. "Tell us of this Deep Magic."

"Tell you?" said the Witch, her voice growing suddenly shriller. "Tell you what is written on the very Table of Stone which stands beside us? . . . You at least know the Magic which the Emperor put into Narnia at the very beginning. You know that every traitor belongs to me as my lawful prey and that I have a right to a kill."[5]

The Witch and Aslan talk among themselves and Aslan then announces that the Witch has renounced her claim on Edmund.

Aslan instructs Peter to prepare for the Witch and her people to attack Peter and the good creatures of Narnia. Aslan sorrowfully journeys, with Susan and Lucy, to the Stone Table. Aslan is set upon by the Witch's creatures. He is shaved, muzzled, bound, and mocked. The Witch taunts Aslan, telling him that his death will not save Edmund. After Aslan dies, she will kill Edmund and the others. Aslan dies. Susan and Lucy mournfully care for Aslan's body. As they are leaving, there are wild colors in the sky and then a great CRACK sound. The Stone Table is broken and Aslan has come back to life.

"But what does it all mean?" asked Susan . . . .

"It means," said Aslan, "that though the Witch knew the Deep Magic there is a magic deeper still which she did not know. Her knowledge goes back only to the dawn of time. But if she could have looked a little further back into the stillness and the darkness before Time dawned, she would have known that when a willing victim who has committed no treachery was killed in a traitor's stead, the Table would crack and Death itself would start working backwards."[6]

Aslan brings the two sisters with him to the Witch's palace. Aslan breaths on the creatures who had been turned into stone; they come back to life. The gates of the structure are destroyed. The myriad of freed creatures joins together with Aslan to meet

5. Lewis, *Chronicles*, 175.
6. Lewis, *Chronicles*, 185.

up with Peter and his forces, who are in a pitched, desperate battle with the Witch and her army. Aslan and the Narnian creatures are victorious over the Witch. Much happens that you will discover when you find time to read the rest, involving rejoicing, feasting, a coronation, and eventually the return of the four siblings to our world.

Let us consider four objections to the conflict between good and evil in *Lion.*

First objection: Isn't there a problem with inventing a world ruled over by a tyrannical Witch? Why create a world with such unbridled cruelty?

Reply: It is supposed to be a problem. There is a backstory about the origin of evil in Narnia that is given in *Magician,* but in *Lion* all we know is that the Witch is a descendent of Lilith (a demonic figure from Jewish myth) and not fully human. This may bring up the classic problem of evil (why is there any evil at all?), but inventing a world in which there is tyranny and oppression is inventing a world very much like our own.[7] Moreover, as G. K. Chesterton points out, one of the important elements in fairytales is that they can provide us with a way of envisaging the defeat of evil:

> Fairy tales, then, are not responsible for producing in children fear, or any of the shapes of fear; fairy tales do not give the child the idea of the evil or the ugly; that is in the child already, because it is in the world already. Fairy tales do not give the child his first idea of bogey. What fairy tales give the child is his first clear idea of the possible defeat of bogey. The baby has known the dragon intimately ever since he had an imagination. What the fairy tale provides for him is a St. George to kill the dragon.
>
> Exactly what the fairy tale does is this: it accustoms him for a series of clear pictures to the idea that these limitless terrors had a limit, that these shapeless enemies have enemies in the knights of God, that there is

---

7. I address the problem of evil in multiple publications, but see especially the *Cascade Companion to Evil.*

something in the universe more mystical than darkness, and stronger than strong fear.[8]

The *Chronicles* give us the means of understanding how terrible, dreaded forces can be overcome by divinely empowered life.

Second objection: Isn't there something wrong in the story with the claim that every traitor belongs to the Witch as her rightful prey? Doesn't this mean that the Witch has a right over Edmund? "A right to a kill"? In our world, one of the reasons why some governments do not negotiate with terrorists is that such negotiation can be seen as legitimizing the terrorists. Does the agreement between Aslan and the Witch imply that the Witch has some legitimate authority? Does it even enhance her prestige that Aslan yields to her?

Reply: On the Witch's claim that all of Narnia will perish if her right over Edmund is not upheld, keep in mind that *Lion* is very much in the tradition of fairytales in which there is some condition set for the existence of a realm. As G. K. Chesterton observes:

> If you really read the fairy-tales, you will observe that one idea runs from one end of them to the other—the idea that peace and happiness can only exist on some condition. This idea, which is the core of ethics, is the core of the nursery-tales. The whole happiness of fairy-land hangs upon a thread, upon one thread. Cinderella may have a dress woven on supernatural looms and blazing with unearthly brilliance; but she must be back when the clock strikes twelve. The king may invite fairies to the christening, but he must invite all the fairies or frightful results will follow. Bluebeard's wife may open all doors but one. A promise is broken to a cat, and the whole world goes wrong. A promise is broken to a yellow dwarf, and the whole world goes wrong. A girl may be the bride of the God of Love himself if she never tries to see him; she sees him, and he vanishes away. A girl is given a box on condition she does not open it; she opens it, and all the evils of this world rush out at her. A man and woman are put in a garden on condition that they do

8. Chesterton, "On Fairy Tales."

not eat one fruit: they eat it, and lose their joy in all the fruits of the earth.[9]

In *Lion*, the condition at issue involves the penalty for being a traitor, the cost of betraying what is good, and placing oneself in the service of evil. On this front, *Lion* appears to be a fairytale in good company.

But is the fairytale condition in *Lion* fair? Assessing this objection requires we reflect on what kind of right the Witch might have. I propose that the "right" that the Witch claims cannot lie in a decree from Aslan or the Emperor-beyond-the Sea. We do not see any such decree in the founding of Narnia in *Magician*. In *Lion*, the Witch says, "He [Aslan] knows that unless I have blood as the Law says, all Narnia will be overturned and perish in fire and blood."[10] Aslan confirms that what the Witch says is "very true."

But what grounds the precept that the Witch makes: "Every traitor belongs to me as my rightful prey"?[11] I suggest that it cannot lie in the will of Aslan and the Emperor *because the Witch herself is a traitor.* In *Magician*, we see the Witch seeking to kill or injure Aslan and her seeking to dominate all of Narnia; surely this is itself treachery. And if so, the Witch would have the duty (or the right) to execute herself. Moreover, note how Aslan banishes the Witch from Narnia, having a tree planted that will shield Narnia from her. Aslan praises Digory for planting a tree that will prevent the Witch from entering Narnia. While the tree flourishes it will foster a healthy joy for Narnians, while it will keep the Witch from coming within a hundred miles from the Kingdom.

The banishment of the Witch is decisive evidence that the Witch's "right" does not stem from Aslan or the Emperor. So, where does the so-called right come from? In what may be called the *Narnian free-will defense,* I believe that it is reasonable to suppose that, according to "the Law," Aslan gives free will to the

9. Chesterton, "On Fairy Tales."
10. Lewis, *Chronicles*, 176.
11. Lewis, *Chronicles*, 175.

creatures of Narnia.[12] The Law essentially holds that the freedom of creatures is of foundational importance in Narnia. On the view I am proposing, no one is to serve Aslan by force; if creatures willingly side with the Witch, and they themselves become traitors, they have ceded their lives to the Witch, as Edmund did. Edmund becomes a willing servant of the Witch. He pledges to perform what "Your Majesty" (his term) desires, and to be raised in her house to become her heir. Recall that he is promised by the Witch to be a prince and then a king and he accepts this. In the story, then, Edmund has *placed himself in bondage to the Witch*. Others who commit treachery may similarly come to belong to the Witch in virtue of them giving themselves to the Witch. According to the Narnian free-will defense, the Law should be understood as attesting to the high value placed on the freedom of creatures. Creatures may freely serve Aslan (forever) or the Witch (for a time, perhaps believing that the Witch will grant her servants everlasting life).

In terms of the Witch's status in Narnia, note the minor role of the Witch in Deep Magic. Aslan says, "when a willing victim who has committed no treachery is killed in a traitor's stead the Table would crack and Death itself would start working backward."[13] *There is no hint that there needs to be a pact according to which the Witch agrees to the substitution, nor that the Witch would crack the Table or work Death backwards.* Moreover, at the risk of some repetition, it is abundantly clear that the power of freeing a traitor (or Edmund) does not lie in the arrangement (or "pact") with the Witch, as that is not only not in "the Law" cited by the Witch, but in the following event we see that there was no real bona fide promise, but merely the pretense of a binding agreement. The Witch says to Aslan:

> And now, who has won? Fool, did you think that by
> all this you would save the human traitor? Now I will
> kill you instead of him as our pact was and so the Deep
> Magic will be appeased. But when you are dead what will
> prevent me from killing him as well? And who will take

12. See Lewis, *Chronicles*, 80.
13. Lewis, *Chronicles*, 185.

him out of my hand then? Understand that you have given me Narnia forever, you have lost your own life and not saved his. In that knowledge, despair and die.[14]

The Witch is a traitor not just to Aslan, the Emperor, and Narnia, but she has betrayed or violated Deep Magic itself.

In *Magician*, we have additional reasons to not be impressed by the Witch: Aslan appears to be invulnerable to physical harm (the Witch hurls a metal rod at Aslan intending to injure or kill him, but she fails to do so) and not to enter into bargains. Note here that if indeed Aslan by nature is invulnerable to physical harm, then his dying would amount to his setting aside such invulnerability, making his death a *voluntary* submission. And returning to bargains, many philosophers would not see any arrangement of two parties to a promise as a genuine exchange of promises unless both parties are sincere.[15] It is evident in the story that the Witch has no intention of sparing Edmund from death. And this is apparently evident to Aslan or he would not have bothered warning Peter that the Witch will attack him and the good creatures of Narnia. I suggest that all this strengthens our recognizing the depth of Aslan's love for Edmund. Aslan so loved Edmund that he allowed himself to be killed in order to bring life out of death and, in so doing, exposed the sham nature of the Witch as a liar and murderer.

Third objection: Why did Aslan agree to take Edmund's place? Why not just kill the Witch and free Edmund?

Reply: Aslan agrees to take Edmund's place so that the Witch would renounce her claim over Edmund. This does amount to

14. Lewis, *Chronicles*, 181.

15. On this view, if you promise to pay someone for loaning you their car, but you have no intention of returning the car, you have not made a genuine promise. Rather, you are simply trying to convince your victim that you made a promise, perhaps in the course of attempting to steal their vehicle. In the literature on promises, this is called an *illusory promise* (or the illusion of a promise) or acting in bad faith (essentially, lying). A famous case of a sham promise is the German-Soviet Nonaggression Pact on August 23, 1938, when Germany and the USSR agreed to not take military action against each other for ten years. Germany had no intention to abide by this agreement, as it became apparent to the Soviet Union when Germany launched Operation Barbarossa in 1941.

what appears to be a straightforward payment or ransom to the Witch (even though her lack of sincerity undermines there being an authentic promise on her part), but this is only part of the story that involves a greater context in which the payment is made. *Aslan pays the cost of what it takes to remove the effects of Edmund's treachery and secure his willing liberation from the Witch's power. Aslan needed to overturn the Witch's reign of death by bringing life out of death (or, as it were, to make death work backwards). By his taking Edmund's place, he absorbs the penalty of Edmund's evil and reverses the powerful cycle of evil which involves a tyranny in which any resistance to the Witch ends in death.* The self-absorbed desire by Edmund for personal satiation and power is challenged and overturned by Aslan's loving self-offering, his resurrection, and bringing to life the creatures whom the Witch had turned to stone. In the story, Mr. Beaver was right that only Aslan can truly rescue Edmund, and the other victims, because only Aslan can overcome the death spread by the Witch and turn Edmund and the others back to loyalty, life, and goodness.

The objector might persist: But why should Aslan die rather than exercise power—perhaps omnipotence—simply to destroy the Witch? Or even to destroy death? Which, incidentally, does not happen in the story; presumably people continue to die in Narnia after Aslan's resurrection, even if they are utterly innocent.

In authoring *Lion,* Lewis had yet to work up an eschatology (a view of last things like death and life after death) for Narnia, and so Aslan's resurrection in the story is not seen as the final (as it were) defeat of death. But the genius of the ransom theory in the story is that *Aslan enters into the prison of death and sin in order to lead the captive to freedom, to show the way to new life.* It is sometimes not enough in a rescue operation to destroy the gates to a prison or a trap. Think of the famous Tham Luang cave rescue in 2018. Twelve members of a football team and their coach were trapped in a cave. Over the course of eighteen days, all thirteen were rescued but only because expert British divers, Thai Navy Seals, and an elite United States Air Force team *went down into the cave to lead them out.* At one point in the rescue, each child was clipped to one of the rescuers, who guided them through the narrow passages to safety. When someone personally enters such a rescue there is a natural bond or solidarity between the rescuer and those rescued. After his resurrection, and Aslan brings back to life the talking creatures whom the Witch had turned to stone, note the great bond between Aslan and those who have been restored to life. A lion is overwhelmed when Aslan referred to him in the phrase "Us Lions": "Did you hear what he said? *Us Lions.* That means him and me. *Us Lions.* That's what I like bout Aslan. No side, no stand-off-ishness. *Us Lions.*"[16]

Just as the thirteen trapped footballers in Tham Luang had to follow their rescuers out of the cave, so too the pathway to freedom from servitude and death in Narnia is by following the beautiful Aslan, the creator and redeemer of Narnia. There is widespread testimony in Christian tradition of the saving role of alluring, sacred beauty. To cite just one example, see Isaac of Nineveh's account of the power of humility, an account that seems a bit Narnian:

> The humble man confronts murderous wild beasts. From the moment they see him their savagery is tamed, they approach him as if he were their owner, nodding their heads and licking his hands and feet. They actually scent coming from him the fragrance that Adam breathed forth before the Fall when they came to him in paradise and he gave them their names.[17]

To further a reply to the current objection, let's distinguish several types of goods: there are what may be called *salvageable goods*, *compensatory goods*, and then *redemptive goods*. A salvageable good is one that survives a loss; for example, after their marriage ends in divorce, the couple might still engage in the goods of co-parenting and friendship. A compensatory good is one that compensates for some damage; after I spill coffee on your computer I purchase for you a new one, perhaps even better than the one I ruined. What I am referring to as redemptive goods are goods that are transformative and make something damaged a

16. Lewis, *Chronicles*, 190.

17. Isaac of Nineveh, *Ascetic Treatises*, 224.

better, transformed good or value. A plausible redemptive good is the re-union of Lucy and Mr. Tumnus after Aslan has brought the Faun back to life. So, Lucy and Mr. Tumnus met under dire circumstances; Mr. Tumnus was going to kidnap Lucy. He sorrowfully confesses this, aids Lucy in escaping and then is punished by the Witch, who turned him to stone. When Lucy finds Mr. Tumnus, and he is brought back to life by Aslan, Lucy and Mr. Tumnus hold hands and dance together with joy.

What has taken place is not a matter of salvaging or compensating, but of *transformation* from sorrow to joy. This joy emerges in their participating in the course of Aslan's self-offering whereby he demonstrates the stronger power of love and life over against hate and death.

So, back to the question of whether Aslan might not have just used omnipotent power to destroy the Witch, death, and sin: what would be missing is the role that Aslan plays in *personally participating* in the overcoming of the Witch, death, and sin. Such divine participation is the deepest magic in Narnia. In Ancient Greek philosophy, especially Platonism, the notion of participation (the Greek term is *methexis*) was seen as vital: from a Platonic point of view, we should strive to participate in the Good. Just as Edmund's initial participation in the Witch's scheme brought about betrayal and hate, his subsequent participation in the fight against the Witch was restorative. And the same is true of Lucy using her cordial to bring healing to the wounded. They both participate in the redemption of Narnia within the great good of Aslan's participation in their lives and the creatures of Narnia.[18]

To see that the central point of atonement in Narnia is chiefly the evident cost to Aslan of turning death into life, see Aslan's bringing Prince Caspian back to life in the last chapter of *Voyage*. Caspian is restored to life by Aslan's blood, when this blood is not offered to a Witch or any other demonic being.

---

18. The aptness of using a military metaphor in describing God's participating with us in the atonement is supported in Gunton, *The Actuality of Atonement*. For an outstanding book on the nature of participation as a vital element in Christianity, see Davison, *Participation in God*.

Fourth objection: Didn't Aslan deceive the Witch? Isn't that wrong? This has been addressed earlier, but because of its historic role in the rejection of the ransom theory, let us consider the matter further.

Reply: Wrongful deception involves misleading or concealing from someone a truth when they deserve or have a right to that truth. You commit wrongful deception if you are a doctor prescribing medicine and fail to inform patients of dangerous side-effects (for example, a high risk of addiction leading to overdosing); you are also in the wrong even if an innocent person asks you the time and (perhaps for the sake of your own entertainment) you deliberately mislead them. In *Lion,* given their agreement, the Witch may have deserved or had a right to know that when she killed Aslan, he died. She was not deceived that the torture of Aslan caused him very real pain. In such matters, she was not misled. I suggest it would be preposterous to suppose that the murderous Witch deserved or had a right to know that Aslan's death would not be *permanent and irreversible.* We might well say the Witch made a miscalculation: she thought that by killing Aslan the path would be open for her and her army to kill Edmund, Peter, Susan, Lucy, and all the good creatures of Narnia. But this involved a failure in her own planning—an underestimation of the power of Aslan, not a matter of Aslan wrongly concealing a truth or deliberately lying.

Think of any commonplace merely human assault that takes place when an assailant has miscalculated the resources of a victim. Imagine that a wicked person has given you a poisoned drink, intending to kill you, but unknown to them you possess an antidote and use it successfully. What possible circumstance (other than you desiring your own demise) might lead you to point out to the assailant that they should use a different, more effective poison? I will return to the charge of deception in the next chapter when engaging the Gregorian ransom theory. As noted in the introduction while I propose there is zero deception of the Witch in Narnia, some early Christians, such as Gregory of Nyssa, thought it fitting that God would deceive Satan. I will offer some reasons in the next chapter why such "deception" is defensible and in line

with biblical portraits of good versus evil. But, to rep... see no
deception or lying or dishonesty of any kind by Aslan ...ion and
the other *Chronicles*.

In *Lion*, Susan and Lucy do not immediately ... Edmund
about the cost of his freedom, but in other stories ... and and
others seem well aware of the cost to Aslan of the rans... In *Voyage*, Edmund knows only too well about the cracked ... e Table
and the instrument used in Aslan's death.

Let us address elements of the atonement in the o... r *Chronicles*. In *Caspian* the main theme is the restoration of ... ia after
a hostile invasion by the Telmarines. This might be s... as a kind
of atonement insofar as it involves bringing togeth... e good,
surviving Narnians in unity with Aslan, a process th... nvolves,
in the end, restoring order by sending most of the Tel... ines out
of Narnia to a new homeland. The Pevensie children ... e to the
aid of the rightful King of Narnia, Prince Caspian, w... is being
hunted by his usurper uncle Miraz. The children, Casp... and the
good Narnians gather at Aslan's How, which includ... e Stone
Table. Nikabrik, a treacherous dwarf, seeks to summo... e White
Witch but is defeated and destroyed. Aslan's party is ... ious in
combat, including single combat between Peter and ... raz, with
the aid of warrior trees and a river god.

In *Caspian*, there is one element of death working ... wards.
Near the beginning of the story, Caspian is first told ... t Aslan
and the old Narnia by his nurse. His wicked uncle b... ishes the
nurse. But, after the defeat of the Telmarines in battle. ... an finds
her, restores her health, and then reunites her with C... ian.[19] In
this scene, Aslan is almost the embodiment of life itsel... preading
life to life.

In *Voyage*, Lucy, Edmund, and a new charact... Eustace
Scrubb, are magically taken to Narnia through a pai... g, finding themselves aboard the Narnian ship, the *Dawn ...der, under the leadership of Caspian, now the King of Nar... Eustace
is a spoiled, self-centered chap who is transformed to ... lth and
the good through Aslan, who uses a kind of intimat... mbling

19. Lewis, *Chronicles*, 409.

34

surgery. There is one key reference to the atonement in *Lion*, which is worthy of notice. When the Dawn Treader reaches "The Beginning of the End of the World," Caspian and others come across "Aslan's Table" on which there is a "Knife of Stone," in the care of Ramandu, a retired star, and his daughter, referred to in this exchange as "the girl":

> "What is this Knife of Stone? asked Eustace.
> "Do none of you know it?" said the girl.
> "I –I think," said Lucy, "I've seen something like it before. It was a knife like it that the White Witch used when she killed Aslan at the Stone Table long ago."
> "It was the same," said the girl, "and it was brought here to be kept in honour while the world lasts."[20]

As this exchange is so short, it is difficult to extrapolate a great deal, but a natural interpretation is that what is being honored is not the knife itself, but Aslan's submitting to the knife. The knife was used as a terrible instrument of death in the course of Aslan's being tortured and killed. But after the resurrection and defeat of the White Witch, the knife has become something like a spoil of war, a token to remind us of Aslan's atoning sacrifice and victory.

There are a great number of theologically interesting elements in *Chair*, to be investigated in chapter five. Connecting with atonement in Narnia, there is a powerful witch who kills King Caspian's wife, the mother of their son Rillian, and holds Rillian hostage by an evil spell as her servant. Rillian is released from his captivity assisted by two children (Eustace and Jill) sent by Aslan along with Puddleglum (a beloved, faithful, heroic but gloomy Marshwiggle) when Rillian destroys the chair in which he is chained (during periods when the Witch's enchantment abates and Rillian is in his right mind) and the Witch is destroyed. There is no ransom involved in Rillian's liberation, but in the resurrection of Rillian's father, the instrument or means of the restoration of King Caspian is the blood of Aslan. As noted above, the blood is a ransom, but not paid to a witch or any other evil creature. It is a ransom insofar

---

20. Lewis, *Chronicles*, 518.

as it is *the price or cost that is paid by Aslan to bring life out of death.* This is a clear case when the term "ransom" is being used to identify a cost paid for release from death, as opposed to a price paid to a kidnapper or hostage-taker.[21] Here is the event:

> Then Aslan stopped and the children looked into the stream. And there, on the golden gravel of the stream, lay King Caspian, dead, with the water flowing over him like liquid glass. His long white beard swayed in it like water weed. And all three stood and wept. Even the Lion wept tears, each tear more precious than the Earth would be if it was a single diamond. And Jill noticed that Eustace looked neither like a child crying, nor like a boy crying and wanting to hide it, but like a grown-up crying. At least, that is the nearest she could get to it; but really, as she said, people don't seem to have any particular ages on that mountain [the Mountain of Aslan, beyond the world in which Narnia lies].
>
> "Son of Adam," said Aslan, "go into that thicket and pluck the thorn that you will find there, and bring it to me."
>
> Eustace obeyed. The thorn was a foot long and sharp as a rapier.
>
> "Drive it into my paw, Son of Adam," said Aslan, holding up his right fore-paw and spreading out the great pad towards Eustace.
>
> "Must I?" Eustace said.
>
> "Yes," said Aslan.
>
> Then Eustace set his teeth and drove the thorn into the Lion's pad. And there came out a great deep drop of blood, redder than all redness you have ever seen or imagined. And it splashed into the stream over the dead body of the King. At the same moment the doleful music stopped. And the dead King began to be changed.

21. In Scripture it is not unusual to refer to the blood of Christ as redeeming or ransoming but without any hint of the blood being offered to Satan, e.g., "A Song to the Lamb" (*Dignus es*) in Revelations 5:9–10, "Worthy art thou [the Lamb] to take the scroll and to open its seals, for thou wast slain and by thy blood didst ransom men for God from every tribe and tongue and people and nation, and hast made them a kingdom and priests to our God, and they shall reign on earth."

His white beard turned to grey, and from grey to yellow, and got shorter and vanished altogether; and his sunken checks grew round and fresh, and the wrinkles were smoothed, and his eyes opened, and his eyes and lips both laughed, and suddenly he leaped up and stood before them—a very young man, or a boy. And he rushed to Aslan and flung his arms as far as they would go round the huge neck, and he gave Aslan the strong kisses of a king, and Aslan gave him the wild kisses of a Lion.[22]

I think that is the most stunning story of resurrection I know of in any fairytale or novel.

Horse is a great tale of two talking horses (Bree and Hwin) and two children (Shasta and Aravis) who seek freedom from enslavement and a dreadful arranged marriage. There is some allusion to the atonement in *Lion*. Bree refers to Aslan as "the great deliverer of Narnia who drove away the Witch and the Winter."[23] Two other elements in *Horse* bear on atonement in Narnia.

First, there is stress on the reality of Aslan. He asks Bree to draw near to him: "'Now, Bree,' he said, 'you poor, proud frightened Horse, draw near. Nearer still, my son. Do not dare not to dare. Touch me. Smell me. Here are my paws, here is my tail, these are my whiskers. I am a true Beast.'"[24] This bears on atonement insofar as it reinforces the idea that Aslan is not a mere metaphor or idea. Atonement takes place with a real Lion, involving real suffering, death, and resurrection.

Second, there is some suggestion that redemption or moral transformation requires that wrongdoers take seriously the harm they do. This is significant, as we shall see in chapter three when we address the practice of forgiveness. Some Christians hold that forgiveness needs (in part) to be preconditioned by the wrongdoer's awareness of the wrong done, whereas others do not. In the course of Aravis escaping from her home, she used her stepmother's slave in a ruse that would allow Aravis to successfully get away, while

22. Lewis, *Chronicles*, 660–61.

23. Lewis, *Chronicles*, 298.

24. Lewis, *Chronicles*, 299.

realizing that the slave would probably undergo some punishment. Near the end of the book, Aslan reveals that he caused Aravis some harm in her journey to Narnia. He tells her he did so in order for her to know what the suffering felt like that she had inflicted on her stepmother's slave.

Aravis' earlier contempt or at least low regard for the slave crumbles. In chapter three I concede that forgiveness can be preemptive and not require full confession, but for full reconciliatory forgiveness to occur, confession (and other elements like repentance) are essential.

In *Magician*, we learn about the creation of Narnia and we get the backstory on the Witch, the Professor, the lamppost that the Pevensie children see when they first come to Narnia, and the wardrobe, all of which play such vital roles in *Lion*.

Two children, Digory and Polly, travel with magic rings to different worlds. In one dreadful realm, Charn, royal looking people appear as statues. There is a bell with a rune challenging anyone who comes upon it, to strike it. Digory is drawn to striking it, while Polly resists. They quarrel with vehemence, especially Digory. In an almost violent act, forcefully subduing Polly, Digory strikes the bell. It brings only one of the stone creatures to life, Queen Jadis (who later becomes the White Witch), who rescues the children from the collapsing building only to reveal herself as the destroyer of all life on Charn, except her own, after a ferocious war with her sister. She appears to have no conscience whatever, and no regret at the immense killing and even the loss of life of her own warriors. In this account, then, we learn that the roots of evil precede the creation of Narnia and that the awakening of evil lies with Digory, a Son of Adam. Parts of this story will be addressed in chapter five.

In *Magician*, much happens between our world and Narnia, but in terms of atonement in Narnia, at least four elements stand out.

First, it appears that in Narnia, evil (or the Witch) does not have the power to create worlds, only to destroy them. And the Witch is powerless in preventing Aslan in creating a world. As

Aslan is creating Narnia through singing, he is walking slowly when the Witch assaults him with an iron bar that she had taken from a lamppost back in London. The Witch hits Aslan straight in the face, but to no effect. The heavy metal bar bounces off of Aslan, who continues his walking, continuing his act of creation.[25]

Uncle Andrew, an eccentric, but somewhat nasty character, suggests it would be good to kill the Lion with a gun, but Digory reproves him. If the Lion didn't mind getting hit by an iron bar, why think being shot by a gun would be more effective? The iron that Jadis throws actually becomes planted in the ground and starts growing into a lamppost. The power of Aslan to create life seems to foreshadow how he is able to surmount death in *Lion*. It also suggests (as noted earlier) that when the Witch kills Aslan in *Lion*, she would not have been able to do this unless Aslan willfully made himself vulnerable.

Second, while Aslan announces to the new creatures of Narnia that evil has come into Narnia by a son of Adam (Digory), Aslan himself will bear the worst cost (the ransom) in overcoming evil.

> "You see, friends," [Aslan] said, "that before the new, clean world I gave you is seven hours old, a force of evil has already entered it; waked and brought hither by this son of Adam." . . . "But do not be cast down," said Aslan, still speaking to the Beasts. "Evil will come of that evil, but it is still a long way off, and I will see to it that the worst falls on myself."[26]

Though the text is not explicit about this, clearly Aslan is foretelling the events in *Lion*.

Third, *Magician* furthers the theme of the redemptive triumph of life over death. As Digory brought evil into Narnia, he is charged by Aslan to undertake a quest that will ultimately lead to a magical protective force against evil and also lead to the restoration to life of his ill mother. With the aid of Polly and a winged horse, Digory is flown to a garden where he is to take an

25. Lewis, *Chronicles*, 66.
26. Lewis, *Chronicles*, 80.

apple and return with it to offer to Aslan. He is tempted by the Witch to consume the apple himself to gain everlasting life or to use the apple himself to restore his mother's life. He removes the Witch and gives the apple to Aslan, who bids him plant the apple in Narnia. Digory does so and it grows into a tree that will protect Narnia for ages. Being a magical tree in Narnia, it grows and bears fruit immediately. Aslan instructs Digory to take an apple from the tree back to his world to bring recovery to his mother. Indeed, the mother's health does return, as Aslan had said. Life (contained in the apple) puts death to flight.

Fourth, while in the introduction I characterized the ransom theory of the atonement as the victory of life over death in *Magician* it is quite clear that life alone is not itself redemptive. The Witch eats the magical fruit and will therefore live forever (unless she is killed), but this length of life is not itself good. It is life in the presence of Aslan that is joyfully redemptive, not life grounded on the craving for domination.

The last of the *Chronicles*, *Battle*, contains multiple fascinating events, including those involving deception and the exposure of deception, battle, the epic conclusion of the history of Narnia since its creation, the opening of a gate to the true Narnia, last judgment, being in relationship with Aslan without serving it, and the journey into Aslan's own country. The ending of *Battle* speaks to what Chesterton describes as the great longing of childhood, the "longing for larger and larger horizons."[27] According to Chesterton, this longing usually proceeds from image to image. "The imagination is supposed to work towards the infinite, though in that sense the infinite is the opposite of the imagination. For the imagination deals with an image, and an image is in its nature a thing that has an outline, and therefore a limit."[28] That is what we find in the majestic succession of image after image in chapter 14 of *Battle*, "Farewell to Shadowland." We come across a change between Lucy and Mr. Tumnus, then we see Reepicheep, then Aslan, then a cascade of more images stretching out beyond what we

27. Chesterton, "The Romance of Childhood," 251.
28. Chesterton, "The Romance of Childhood," 251.

are told will never end. This is truly an exalted view of an endless participatory good, the fruition of at-one-ment and attunement of creatures and Aslan.

Time in Narnia is different from time in our world. In terms of earthly time, Narnia lasted only fifty-two years, but in terms of years in Narnian time, it lasted 2,555 years with many generations of creatures.

I believe we have covered enough ground in this chapter to turn from the ransom that occurs in Narnia to address the ransom theory in Christian theology. Allow me to summarize the results of this chapter. The ransom story in Narnia has been criticized for its having the Witch as a character at all (why invent a world with such a tyrant?); even if it is acceptable to have such an evil character, some argue that the *Chronicles* give too much status and power to the Witch; the *Chronicles* leaves unexplained why Aslan would give his life for Edmund; and the ransom offered by Aslan involves him deceiving the Witch. I have replied that having an imaginary world with a tyrant is indeed a problem, just as having tyrants in our own world is a problem. I commend Chesterton's view that fairytales aid us in imagining how great evils may be overcome, a view shared by Lewis. The Witch's status and power is tenuous. She lacks the sincerity to actually form a proper legal bargain with Aslan; her lying that she would spare Edmund in exchange for Aslan renders her words about renunciation null and void in terms of ethics or law. Any claim that the Witch has a right or duty to kill traitors involves her in the absurd position of having an obligation to kill herself because she herself is a traitor to Aslan and the Emperor. This is evident in *Lion*, but especially clear in *Magician*. Her power over Aslan seems contingent on Aslan voluntarily shedding his invulnerability. Aslan gives his life for Edmund, not in virtue of a bargain, but in a display of love whereby he voluntarily assumes the cost (ransom) of death and sin, in order to bring life out of death. Aslan is involved in no deception of any kind. He truly offers himself to suffering and death, and truly suffers and dies. Aslan's resurrection makes no sense unless this is so. The Witch underestimated the power of Aslan to "turn death backwards," but

Aslan was under no obligation or rightful expectation to inform the Witch that his death would not be permanent and irreversible.

Before turning to Christian theology, let us consider one, rather public, last complaint about Lewis' treatment of Queen Susan in *Battle* raised by the fantasy writers Philip Pullman, J. K. Rowling, and others. The issue involves an aspect of atonement insofar as it involves Susan not being at one with Aslan at the end. Susan does not reach Narnia or Aslan's country in the last volume in the *Chronicles*. Here is an exchange between the current (and last) King of Narnia, Tirian, and Peter, Eustace, Jill, and Polly:

> "Sire," said Tirian, when he had greeted all three, "if I read the chronicles aright, there should be another. Has not your Majesty two sisters? Where is Queen Susan?"
>
> "My sister Susan," answered Peter shortly and gravely, "is no longer a friend of Narnia."
>
> "Yes," said Eustace, "and whenever you've tried to get her to come and talk about Narnia or do anything about Narnia, she says 'What wonderful memories you have! Fancy your still thinking about all those funny games we used to play when we were children.'"
>
> "Oh, Susan!" said Jill. "She's interested in nothing nowadays except nylons and lipstick and invitations. She always was a jolly too keen on being grown-up."
>
> "Grown-up, indeed, said Lady Polly. "I wish she *would* grow up. She wasted all her school time wanting to be the age she is now, and she'll waste all the rest of her life trying to stay that age. Her whole idea is to race on to the silliest time of one's life as quick as she can and then stop there as long as she can."[29]

Objection: Is there something vile the way Susan is written out of the *Chronicles*? Let's put the objection about the treatment of Susan in the strongest possible terms: Did Lewis kill Susan?

Reply: It may not be absurd to think of authors killing one of their characters. A plausible case would be Arthur Conan Doyle's "The Final Problem" in 1893; Sherlock Homes falls to his death. Actually, in an 1891 letter to his mother, Doyle wrote about

---

29. Lewis, *Chronicles*, 741.

slaughtering Holmes. But the idea that authors whose characters die are killers boarders on the absurd, otherwise Shakespeare should be deemed a mass-killer. It may be that Lewis was like some writers, such as Tolkien, who believed that his characters had minds of their own. Tolkien professed to be surprised and dismayed that Gollum turned out as he did. Be that as it may, Lewis addressed Susan's plight in a 1955 letter to a girl:

> Peter gets back to Narnia in it. I am afraid Susan does not. Haven't you noticed in the two [Narnia books, *Lion* and *Caspian*] you have read that she is rather fond of being too grownup? I am sorry to say that side of her got stronger and she forgot about Narnia.
> The books don't tell us what happened to Susan. She is left alive in this world at the end, having been turned into a rather silly, conceited young woman. But there is plenty of time for her to mend, and perhaps she will get to Aslan's country in the end—in her own way. I think that whatever she had seen in Narnia she *could* (if she was the sort that wanted to) persuade herself, as she grew up, that it was "all nonsense."[30]

So, Lewis is innocent of the charge of killing Susan; after all, she is still alive at the end of the *Chronicles*. On the contrary, the way her siblings get to Narnia is on the occasion of them (not Susan) being killed in a train wreck. I suggest Susan's falling-out with Narnia keeps the *Chronicles* from being too Pollyanna. She might even represent some philosophers I know who dismiss the *Chronicles* as *mere* fairytales, fit only for children. While those philosophers may or may not be keen about nylons and lipstick, they assume they are too grown-up to philosophically engage in what we might learn in Narnia. In a sense, Susan has given herself over to fashion, but it should be appreciated that there can be a danger of giving oneself over to *philosophical fashions*. Bertrand Russell offers this sarcastic-laden warning about fashion:

---

30. Found online at: https://www.narniaweb.com/2021/08/what-c-s-lewis -said-about-susans-fate-in-the-last-battle/.

The belief that fashion alone should dominate opinion has great advantages. It makes thought unnecessary and puts the highest intelligence within the reach of everyone. It is not difficult to learn the correct use of such words as "complex," "sadism," "Oedipus," "bourgeois," "deviation," "left"; and nothing more is needed to make a brilliant writer or talker. Some, at least, of such words represented such thought on the part of their inventors, like paper money they were originally convertible into gold. But they have become for most people inconvertible, and in depreciating have increased nominal wealth in ideas. And so we are enabled to despise the paltry fortunes if former times.[31]

So philosophical fashions have their limits, as I suppose there are limits to cosmetics.

Objection: Might Lewis have not included Susan in Aslan's company because of her maturing into a sexually active woman? This seems to be a part of the concern of Philip Pullman and J. K. Rowling.

Reply: In my view, that is preposterous, or at least a hypothesis that goes well beyond any textual evidence. In *Horse*, the problem with Susan marrying Prince Rabadash has nothing to do with misgivings about Susan being sexually united with the Prince. If Lewis was skittish about Susan being sexual, why entertain such a courtship in the first place? The engagement is not cut off because Susan (and presumably, Lewis the author) has misgivings about being sexually active! I have yet to find any qualms about sex in the *Chronicles*; presumably Caspian and his wife have to make love in order for them to have a son; and, similarly, Shasta and Aravis had to have sex together in order to procreate. (I am not implying that the function of sex has to be procreative, but, short of artificial insemination, I am assuming that in Narnia sexual union is essential for procreation.) The issue with the lipstick is not about Lewis' discomfort with Susan's sexual maturity but her loss of the ability to be childlike, which leads to her turning away from her life in Narnia.

31. Russell, "On Being Modern-Minded," 352.

In a sense, the book you are currently reading has been written to persuade the Susans of our world to re-consider their younger encounters with things Narnian! If you're out there, Susans of the world, this book is for you.

Chapter Two

A Gregorian Ransom Theory

This chapter is named in honor of Gregory of Nyssa (fourth century), widely recognized as a saint in Roman Catholicism, Eastern Orthodoxy, and Anglicanism. He is credited historically for stressing God's infinitude, especially God's limitless goodness; in fact, he held that it is because of God's maximal boundless goodness that our journey to God will itself be unending. Gregory thereby treats life after death as a dynamic process, not a static state. He had a high view of the goodness of participating in this life here and now. Once we begin to participate in God's life we are on a path that is inexhaustible; just as there is no end point or terminus for God's unlimited love, there will be no terminus for the lives of those in union with God. He would have fully embraced Lewis' depiction of the good of creatures participating with Aslan in the stewardship of Narnia and Aslan participating in the freeing of Edmund and the overcoming of sin and death. He had a high view of God's Triune nature (in Christianity the Godhead is not homogenous but consists of three persons: Father, Son, and Holy Spirit) as a wondrous inner life of love. Gregory viewed the resurrection of Jesus as heralding a universal salvation in which all persons will (ultimately) become sacred or divinized through Christ (*theosis*). He had a high view of free will, likening it to a means by which persons radically create their own characters; in his terms, we can give birth to ourselves.

> Here [in the spiritual realm] birth is not the result of intervention from outside, as happens with bodily creatures who reproduce in an external way. Spiritual birth is the result of free choice, and we are thus, in a sense, our own parents, creating ourselves as we want to be, freely fashioning ourselves according to the pattern of our choice.[1]

There is much to admire in Gregory's fascinating contribution to Christian thought and practice. I am singling him out here as a representative of the early Christian account of the ransom theory involving Satan, partly because I think his views have greater merit than is recognized today.

Gregory defends an all-out supernatural ransom theory in which God lures Satan into taking Jesus as a payment to release us from our bondage to Satan. Jesus then overcomes Satan and

1. Gregory of Nyssa, *Life of Moses* 24.

releases us to a transfigured life with God. In the process, Satan himself comes to be delivered from evil. This chapter has four sections. In the first, let us consider an overview of the biblical and theological context in which Gregory's ransom account was forged. Is the existence of Satan something we can or should take seriously today? Section two lays out Gregory's account of atonement. The third section defends the Gregorian account against objections. A final section offers a reason for preferring the Christus Victor ransom theory over against St. Gregory's.

Brief Overview of Sin, Death, and Satan

With all its complexity, the Bible generally supports the conviction that persons are responsible for their wrongdoing (e.g., Deut 30:15–20). True, one may find passages that suggest God's providence is exacting and comprehensive, involving foreordination, but many, if not most Christian theologians with strong commitments to divine providence contend that this is compatible with recognizing human responsibility for wrongdoing. When you murder (violating the fifth commandment), you are responsible for this wrong.

The narrative of the first humans (Adam and Eve) in Genesis 1–3 is interpreted in very different ways by Christians. Some take it as historical, others as a myth, allegory, parable, or metaphor, and some as a combination, sometimes referred to as mytho-historical. It is difficult to read early Genesis as an exhaustive, non-mythic history. For example, one of the sons of Adam and Eve, Cain, has sexual relations with his wife in Genesis 4:17; where did she come from? Some contemporary Christians who accept evolutionary biology still retain the notion of original sin in two senses: there was probably a first time (or an early era) when humans attained sufficient moral consciousness so that they were able to knowingly judge some of their actions as wrong (or sinful) and, second, there was probably a time (or era) when human ill-doing became entrenched and heritable. Whatever your perspective, the narrative of Eden (or the Edenic or Adamic narrative) seems to show us that the first humans are made in God's image; we were given the garden of Eden by God on the condition that we do not consume fruit from a given tree; Eve was tempted by a serpent to violate God's command to not eat the fruit; both Adam and Eve violate God's command; they are thereby exiled from Eden. What does this mean for the descendants of Adam and Eve?

As the serpent has been interpreted by many Christians as an embodiment of Satan, some Christians have interpreted the early chapters of Genesis as a story of how humans came under the domain (or the domination) of Satan. Such a domain involves captivity to sin and death. Death seems to follow the Adamic sin in Genesis and in chapter 4 we see the first murder between two sons of Adam and Eve. This idea that the first sin brought us under the domain of Satan was then paired by some early theologians with New Testament texts that teach that as sin came into the world through Adam so salvation came into the world through Jesus Christ (Rom 5:12–21). Drawing on New Testament claims that Jesus came to save us from sin and death (Rev 1:18; 21:14; 2 Tim 1:18; John 3:16; 1 Pet 2:24; 3:18; Jas 2:14), Jesus' life—his birth, teaching, miracles, and ultimately his suffering, death by crucifixion, and resurrection—was interpreted by some early Christian theologians as the ransom or cost of our being liberated from the domain or kingdom of Satan. Hebrews 2:14 seems to propose that freeing us from Satan was key to the work of Jesus: "Since therefore the children share in flesh and blood, he [Christ] himself likewise partook of the same things, that through death he might destroy the one who has the power of death, that is, the devil."

The view that Satan is an actual agent receives some support from the Book of Job. Because of the monumental significance of that text, let us briefly pause to consider Satan in that text and make note of its many themes.

In the Book of Job, Satan appears before God to challenge the authenticity of Job's fidelity to God. In chapters 1 and 2, God permits Satan to test Job's faith, which Satan does by bringing about a range of devastating calamities, including the death of Job's children. In terms of the themes in the Book, what makes it the most philosophical text in the Bible is that it raises the problem of evil (if there is an all-good, all-powerful God, why is there evil?); it invites questions about the status of Satan (is Satan a member of God's court?); it includes the notion that merely being (or being alive) can be a great good, a gift from God (Job 1:21); there is a stunning hymn to wisdom (chapter 28); the last chapter may hint at the idea of divine restitution; and the text teaches the lesson that innocent persons such as Job can and do suffer. In a sense, the Book of Job provides theological grounds for Christians to assert that Jesus Christ was innocent and yet suffered profusely. The teaching that in this world those who prosper are not necessarily good and those who suffer and not necessarily evil is a key to the Book. Chesterton draws attention to this teaching:

> Here in this book the question is really asked whether God invariably punishes vice with terrestrial punishment and rewards virtue with terrestrial prosperity. If the Jews had answered that question wrongly they might have lost all their after influence in human history. They might have sunk even down to the level of modern well-educated society. For when once people have begun to believe that prosperity is the reward of virtue, their next calamity is obvious. If prosperity is regarded as the reward of virtue it will be regarded as the symptom of virtue. Men will leave off the heavy task of making good men successful. He will adopt the easier task of making out successful men good.[2]

The famous divine reply to Job in chapters 38–41 might make us inclined to think that, well, if the observable, natural world is so wild, why rule out there being an invisible world of angels and other creatures, perhaps even Satan? As usual, Chesterton has a colorful way of describing God's speech to Job:

> To startle man, God becomes for an instant a blasphemer; one might almost say that God becomes for an instant an atheist. He unrolls before Job a long panorama of created things, the horse, the eagle, the raven, the wild ass,

---

2. Chesterton, "Introduction to the Book of Job."

the peacock, the ostrich, the crocodile. He so describes each of them that it sounds like a monster walking in the sun. The whole is a sort of psalm or rhapsody of the sense of wonder. The maker of all things is astonished at the things he has Himself made.[3]

Could one of the things that God has made be incorporeal, supernatural beings, angels perhaps, some of which are faithful to God, others of which rebel?[4]

In the New Testament, Satan is in dialogue with Jesus in the temptation narratives. Satan appears to be referred to as a "tempter" (Matt 4:3), "the ruler of demons" (Matt 12:24), "the evil one" (1 John 5:18). Jesus addresses Satan in commanding him to be gone (Matt 4:10). Satan is said to fall from heaven (Luke 10:18). Satan enters into Judas (Luke 22:3). In Mark 3:25 Jesus appears to have a philosophy of demons, according to which Satan and his forces have to have some semblance of unity, otherwise they would collapse; "A house divided against itself cannot stand." (It is interesting that in 1858 Abraham Lincoln used this verse about demons in his case for keeping the United States united!) The traditional belief that Satan is a fallen angel was seen as supported by Isaiah 14:12–14 and Ezekiel 28:12–18. While some theologians refer to the aboriginal or Adamic sin as *original sin*, they use the term *primal sin* to refer to the sin of supernatural beings such as those portrayed in Milton's *Paradise Lost*.

To use William James' phrase, is the thesis that Satan exists as a supernatural, wicked being a "live hypothesis" today? For James, a live hypothesis is one that has some appeal to you; it is one that you do not dismiss as impossible or so improbable as to be of no interest (and thus be a dead hypothesis). For many educated

---

3. Chesterton, "Introduction to the Book of Job."

4. I have in mind Satan in the opening scenes of Job. The standard view among biblical scholars is that "the adversary" (the satan) in Job is not quite the same as Satan in the Gospels so much as the seed from which he grew. In Job, satan is a title (hence, *the* satan) and not a name. It refers to the role of testing/accusing assigned to this heavenly being (the accuser). In retrospect, read from a later New Testament perspective, we can see Satan in Job, but the author of Job was not thinking in such terms.

westerners the thesis is probably dead on arrival, but I ⟨...⟩ est that some of the reasoning behind this is suspect. You m⟨...⟩ ule out the existence of incorporeal or immaterial agents if you ⟨...⟩ ow with certainty that scientific naturalism (the view that all ⟨...⟩ t exists can be described or explained in the natural sciences) i ⟨...⟩ true. But many philosophers now object that scientific naturali⟨...⟩ is unable to account for a host of evident phenomena, such a⟨...⟩ bjective experience, values, the normativity of reason, and s⟨...⟩[5] More liberal forms of naturalism also face what seem to be ⟨...⟩ ractable difficulties.[6] Still, in terms of positive reasons to accep⟨...⟩ hat may be called "the Satan hypothesis," probably the hypoth⟨...⟩ is alive largely for those who accept the Bible as divine reve⟨...⟩ on. One might also note that, as observed in the introduction ⟨...⟩ rge percentage of people, including those in the United States ⟨...⟩ believe in spirits and ghosts.[7] But another reason to be at lea⟨...⟩ erested in Satan was identified by C. S. Lewis in his 1942 boo⟨...⟩ *Preface to Paradise Lost*. In the course of Lewis commenting ⟨...⟩ ow it is easier for us to portray Satan (and other creatures wor⟨...⟩ an ourselves) than to portray characters who are better than o⟨...⟩ elves, he refers to "the Satan in us."

> In all but a few writers the "good" characters a⟨...⟩ e
> least successful, and every one who has ever tri⟨...⟩ to
> make even the humblest story ought to know wh⟨...⟩ o
> make a character worse than oneself it is only nec⟨...⟩
> to release imaginatively from control some of th⟨...⟩
> passions which, in real life, are always straining a⟨...⟩ e
> leash; the Satan, the Iago, the Becky Sharp, withi⟨...⟩
> of us, is always there and only too ready, the mome⟨...⟩ e
> leash is slipped, to come out and have in our book⟨...⟩
> holiday we try to deny them in our lives. But if yo⟨...⟩
> to draw a character better than yourself, all you c⟨...⟩
> is to take the best moments you have had and to i⟨...⟩
> ine them prolonged and more consistently embodi⟨...⟩

5. See Goetz and Taliaferro, *Naturalism*.

6. See Copan and Taliaferro, eds., *The Naturalness of Belief*.

7. See https://www.usatoday.com/story/news/nation-no⟨...⟩7/10/25/how-many-people-believe-ghosts-dead-spirits/79421500⟨...⟩.

action. . . . We do not really know what it feels like to be a man much better than ourselves. . . . The Satan in Milton enables him to draw the character well just as the Satan in us enables us to receive it.[8]

So, even if depictions of Satan are not the best guide to describing an actual supernatural, wicked agent, they may be a guide to our darker sides. (Because I think Lewis is highly successful in depicting the character Aslan, it may be reasonable to believe Lewis has an Aslan within.)

One more point deserves to be noted when it comes to Satan or the demonic. It comes from Peter Berger's book *A Rumour of Angels*. Berger identifies areas of life that do not constitute *proofs* of some transcendent, religiously charged realm, but they *hint* at it. One area is our experience of extreme evil. He proposes that some profoundly horrifying events seem to cry out for a judgement that transcends our humanity. He refers to this feeling of absolute condemnation as the *argument from damnation*. By his lights, we can encounter events that we find worthy of damnation or, indeed, cases of damnation. These might well be experiences of what we take to be hell, in the sense of that which is utterly remote from God, a realm of profound malignancy. Our failure to yearn for the absolute condemnation of such events is our failure as human beings. Before citing Berger on this point, it may be useful to consider an example of a profound atrocity. Here is a passage from *The Rape of Nanking: The Forgotten Holocaust of World War II*, in which Iris Chang describes the horrifying treatment of Chinese in the city of Nanking in 1937 and 1938 by Japanese soldiers, resulting in 250,000 to 300,000 deaths.

> Chinese men were used for bayonet practice and in decapitation contests. An estimated 20,000–80,000 Chinese women were raped. Many soldiers went beyond rape to disembowel women, slice off their breasts, nail them alive to walls. Fathers were forced to rape their daughters, and sons their mothers, as other family members watched. Not only did live burials, castration, the carving

8. Hooper, *C. S. Lewis: A Companion & Guide*, 468.

of organs, and the roasting of people become routine, but more diabolical tortures were practiced, such as hanging people by their tongues on iron hooks or burying people to their waists and watching them get torn apart by German shepherds. So sickening was the spectacle that even the Nazis in the city were horrified, one proclaiming the massacre to be the work of "bestial machinery."[9]

According to Berger, it is essential that we see such events as truly, objectively horrifying and damned:

> Indeed, a refusal to condemn in absolute terms would appear to offer prima facie evidence not only of a profound failure in the understanding of justice, but more profoundly of a fatal impairment of *humanitas*. There are certain deeds that cry out to heaven. These deeds are not only an outrage to our moral sense, they seem to violate a fundamental awareness of the constitution of our humanity. In this way, these deeds are not only evil, but *monstrously evil*. . . . No human punishment is "enough" in the case of deeds as monstrous as these. These are deeds that demand not only condemnation, but *damnation* in the full religious meaning of the word—that is, the doer not only puts himself outside the community of men; he also separates himself in a final way from a moral order that transcends the human community, and thus invokes a retribution that is more than human.[10]

This bears on the topic of Satan insofar as we can experience horrors that seem so dehumanizing as to be Satanic or demonic and that call for the damning or condemning by a higher, transcendent power.

> The transcendent element manifests itself in two steps. First, our condemnation is absolute and certain. It does not permit modification or doubt, and it is made in the conviction that it applies to all times and to all men as well as to the perpetrator or putative perpetrator of the

9. Chang, *The Rape of Nanking*, 6.

10. Berger, *A Rumor of Angels*, 66–68.

particular deed. In other words, we give the condemnation the status of a necessary and universal truth.[11]

I am not hereby endorsing Berger's analysis as an argument for theism or for recognizing the demonic, but I propose that he has identified why many of us are prompted to yearn for the reality of an omnibenevolent, omnipotent God to deliver us from evil and, in the place of death and horror, to defeat such evils and redeem the countless victims of demonic forces.

The Ransom Theory of Gregory of Nyssa

I am singling out Gregory as an advocate for a supernatural ransom theory, not because he was the only advocate, but because of his clarity and his significance as a major contributor to Christian theology in general.

As noted earlier, Gregory holds that human persons have free will. This is not the claim that *all* our acts are matters of free choice, but some are, especially when it comes to shaping our characters or our moral and spiritual identity. We were created to pursue the good, the true, and the beautiful, but we abused our freedom and sold ourselves to "the deceiver," Satan.

> We must remember that man was necessarily created subject to change [to better or to worse]. Moral beauty was to be the direction in which his free will was to move; but then he was deceived, to his ruin, by an illusion of that beauty. After we had thus freely sold ourselves to the deceiver, He who of His goodness sought to restore us to liberty could not, because He was just too, for this end have recourse to measures of arbitrary violence. It was necessary therefore that a ransom should be paid, which should exceed in value that which was to be ransomed; and hence it was necessary that the Son of God should surrender Himself to the power of death. God's justice

---

11. Berger, *A Rumor of Angels*, 67.

then impelled Him to choose a method of exchange, as His wisdom was seen in executing it.[12]

Given that he held that human slavery is inherently sinful, it is interesting that Gregory proposes that it would not be just for God simply to free us from slavery. Perhaps the difference between most cases of human slavery and bondage to Satan is that Gregory holds that the former is involuntary, whereas the second is willful. We might also need to appreciate that Gregory's universalism (the view that, in the end, all persons will be saved—atoned, or made "at one" with God) includes Satan (1 Cor 15:28; Phil 2:9–11). From Gregory's point of view, it would be contrary to God's overwhelming loving goodness simply to destroy Satan. Instead, a means must be found to free both humans and Satan from their alienation from God.[13] On this front Lewis' use of the ransom theory in *Lion* is quite different; there is little hope that the Witch will be saved.

The process of liberating us from Satan was for Jesus to take our place. When he did so, Jesus is killed and dies, but then in the resurrection, God through Jesus defeats Satan, sin, and death. Because Satan deceived humankind, God in turn deceived the devil by hiding his Son in human form. Gregory believed that God's deception of the devil was justified not only for our sake, but also for the sake of Satan himself, who would benefit from the incarnation and ransom as well. Gregory partly defends the deception on the grounds that, when Satan himself is saved, he would approve the means of redemption.

> A certain deception was indeed practiced upon the Evil one, by concealing the Divine nature within the human; but for the latter, as himself a deceiver, it was only a just recompense that he should be deceived himself: the great adversary must himself at last find that what has been done is just and salutary, when he also shall experience

the benefit of the Incarnation. He, as well as humanity, will be purged.[14]

Satan fell for God's trick, and saw in Jesus a worthy ransom for all of humanity.

> The Enemy, therefore, beholding in Him such power, saw also in Him an opportunity for an advance, in the exchange, upon the value of what he held. For this reason he chooses Him as a ransom for those who were shut up in the prison of death. But it was out of his power to look on the unclouded aspect of God; he must see in Him some portion of that fleshly nature which through sin he had so long held in bondage. Therefore it was that the Deity was invested with the flesh, in order, that is, to secure that he, by looking upon something congenial and kindred to himself, might have no fears in approaching that supreme power; and might yet by perceiving that power, showing as it did, yet only gradually, more and more splendor in the miracles, deem what was seen an object of desire rather than of fear. Thus, you see how goodness was conjoined with justice, and how wisdom was not divorced from them.

The devil fell for the bait, but the Son of God hidden within proved too powerful for Satan's might to contain or conquer. The power of evil was thus destroyed. Christ's righteousness served as a kind of antidote to evil. The life that was in him overturned the power of death.

> For since, as has been said before, it was not in the nature of the opposing power to come in contact with the undiluted presence of God, and to undergo His unclouded manifestation, therefore, in order to secure that the ransom in our behalf might be easily accepted by him who required it, the Deity was hidden under the veil of our nature, that so, as with ravenous fish, the hook of the Deity might be gulped down along with the bait of flesh,

14. This passage and the following three are taken from Gregory's *Great Catechism*, found at: http://thepropertyofjesus.blogspot.com/2011/03/gregory-of-nyssa-ransom.html/.

> and thus, life being introduced into the house of d ,
> and light shining in darkness, that which is diamet
> opposed to light and life might vanish; for it is not i
> nature of darkness to remain when light is present
> death to exist when life is active.

All of humanity shares in the victory Christ achieved   Satan,
death, and in because he is joined with us through the rnation.

> He stretches forth a hand as it were to prostrate   ,
> and stooping down to our dead corpse He came
> within the grasp of death as to touch a state of dead ,
> and then in His own body to bestow on our natu   e
> principle of the resurrection, raising as He did b
> power along with Himself the whole man. For since
> no other source than from the concrete lump of ou
> ture had come that flesh, which was the receptacle   e
> Godhead and in the resurrection was raised up tog
> with that Godhead, therefore just in the same way
> the instance of this body of ours, the operation of
> the organs of sense is felt at once by the whole syste
> one with that member, so also the resurrection pri   le
> of this member, as though the whole of mankind
> single living being, passes through the entire race,
> imparted from the Member to the whole by virtue
> continuity and oneness of the nature.

A Defense of the Gregorian Ransom T   ry

Is deception always wrong? There are multiple arenas i   ich deception is not only not wrong, it is fully expected and   er. This
is true in sports, games, some forms of entertainme   ar, and
some business practices: it seems fair that American f   ll play-
ers pretend to throw to the left and then throw right; c   nasters
disguise their strategies; magicians divert the attenti   of their
audience to perform a trick; the Allies deceive the G   ns into
thinking that the invasion will take place at Calais; a b   ess firm
may disguise its intent to acquire another company   il it can
undertake the acquisition with maximum profit. Mo   il not all

these cases involve practices in which there are rules, even though the rules of war are notoriously difficult to enforce with precision and consistency. What about hostage negotiations, especially ones that involve the prospects of using deception in a substitution of hostages? Unlike sports, games, entertainment, and business, there is no official, mutually agreed upon handbook, but I suggest that it is hard to rule out the proposal that sometimes deception in, say, hostage substitutions may be commendable.[15]

Imagine you are the justly elected leader of a country facing a rebel force that has kidnapped innocent children. They used deception to get the children by posing as official bus drivers. They offer this bargain: they will release all their captives if you take their place. We can complicate this thought experiment with all kinds of strange suppositions. We can imagine that the rebels are not malevolent and simply want to give you a lecture or we can imagine they intend to humiliate or kill you. Whatever the circumstances, imagine you are an almost superhuman James or Jane Bond, Black Panther or Wonder Woman and yet you tell the hostage takers that you are a gentle lamb who is meek and afraid of your own shadow. The exchange is made. The children are set free. You then overcome your captors. If you like, you can make your victory due, not to your physical prowess, but due to your wit (you overcome your captors with jokes so funny they lapse into semi-conscious states) or other skills (you are a psychological genius who can persuade anyone to do almost anything) or even by your display of love. The latter would definitely fit in well with Gregory's idea that even Satan will be saved by the power of God through Jesus.

Was your concealing your powers in the thought experiment a matter of wrongful deception? I grant that your claim to be a

---

15. Parenthetically, I note that some early Christians subordinated the duty to not lie to the calling to save souls. In the *Sayings of the Desert Fathers*, Abba Alonius advises a monk to lie to a police officer about the whereabouts of a murderer if that might provide an occasion to deliver the murderer to God. "If you do not tell a lie, you are delivering that man to death. It is better that you should hand him over to God, for God knows all things." See Clement, ed., *The Roots of Christian Mysticism*, 286.

meek sheep involves what may ordinarily be called lying, but I propose that what makes lying wrong is when it involves *wrongful deception*. I can wrongly deceive you by telling the truth and not lying at all. Imagine you believe I am a chronic liar and I do not want you to go to the city of Nyssa. You ask me: "Is highway 12 a safe route to Nyssa?" I reply, telling the truth: "It is not. I hear that there are many bandits on that route." Because you think I almost always lie and that I just made up the notion that there are bandits on that highway, you (wrongly) conclude that the route is safe.[16] Back to the thought experiment, I do not think that the kidnappers would have a right to complain about your deception. You did not do to the kidnappers what they did to the children. When they deceived the children, the children deserved the truth. But when you deceived them in the process of negotiating the release of hostages, they were engaged in a grave wrong (kidnapping children) and did not deserve the truth.

Let's consider the merits of the Gregorian ransom theory in the context of replying to four objections: (1) Even if deception is permissible in the above scenario and deception in sports is acceptable, and so on, isn't there still something unfitting about the all-good God engaging in deception? (2) Isn't there something wrong about an innocent person willingly giving themselves over to kidnappers to free others? Maybe it's the least worst plan under the circumstances, but in the above thought experiment isn't it costing you something unfair? (3) Isn't it also unfair that you, an innocent person today, can be subject to a bondage entered into by ancestors? (4) So far, in both chapters and the introduction, sin (or evil or wrongdoing) is linked with death. This is in keeping with the saying, "the wages of sin is death" (Rom 6:23), but is death always bad? Granted, premature (especially violent) death is bad, but isn't dying and death a natural process and simply what is inevitable, given our biology?

---

16. For the difference between lying and deception, see Chisholm, *Ethics and Intrinsic Value*, chapter 6, "The Intent to Deceive."

(1) God and Deception

While it is true that an all-good God would not carry out *wrongful* deception, I do not see that *all* divine deception is forbidden, unwarranted, or unlikely.[17] But because the term "deception" in popular English is almost always used negatively (notwithstanding the role of deception in sports, etc.), consider a term that is more neutral, like *divine hiddenness*.[18] The topic of the *hiddenness of God* is now very popular in philosophy of religion. John Schellenberg has argued for atheism on the grounds that if God exists, God would be more evident to more people, while Christian philosophers like Paul Moser have argued that God's hiddenness is essential for our freedom to seek God by means of spiritual and moral transformation. Moser would be backed up by some outstanding philosophers, like Blaise Pascal and Søren Kierkegaard, Samuel Taylor Coleridge and John Hick, among many others. In terms of the Gregorian ransom theory, imagine that Jesus is offered to Satan in exchange for the freedom of sinners, but Jesus' identity as God incarnate is hidden from Satan. This might be odd if we assume the New Testament should be our guide. Jesus seems to prophesy or predict his resurrection (Mark 9:30–32), some demons seem to know that Jesus is the Son of God (Matt 8:29), some passages (especially in the Gospel of John) seem to imply that Jesus is one with the Father (John 10:30–31), but perhaps Satan (like some contemporary New Testament scholars) is skeptical about all of this and so Jesus' identity and power were hidden (or not apparent) to Satan. Should we bristle at this case of God's hiddenness? If so, we would be ignoring that in the Bible God seems to come close to playing hide and seek. Consider the Song of Songs: the lover (whom commentators usually see as God) is apparent to the beloved (the human soul) and then disappears, then re-appears.

17. Even so, it should be noted that the trustworthiness and reliability of God is a mainstay in Christian Scriptures and philosophy, as seen in Descartes' *Meditations*.

18. In sports, sometimes the word "fake" or "trick play" is used rather than "deception." Hiddenness is in play in non-Abrahamic religions too; in the *Bhagavad Gita*, Krishna is hidden or disguised as a charioteer.

There are thirty-four biblical verses about God hiding (e.g., Deut 31:17–18; Mic 3:4; Ps 30:7). Evil doers are often depicted as acting without foreknowing the outcome of their acts. In the story of Joseph being assaulted by his brothers and sold into slavery, it is later observed that this happened so that God might save the people of Israel through Joseph's authority in Egypt (see Genesis 37–50). Was God wrong to keep this providential purpose hidden? Were the Hebrew midwives wrong to hide the children of Hebrew mothers so that they would not be killed by Pharaoh? Jesus hides some of the meaning of his parables until the end (e.g., all the vineyard parables). When the prophet Nathan confronts David with the charge of adultery, he lures David into making a judgment of condemnation in the case of a person exploiting another, before Nathan then brings David to realize that *he himself* is guilty (2 Sam 12:7–14).

In the introduction, I noted that the ransom theory has sometimes likened Jesus on the cross as a kind of mousetrap, luring Satan into being trapped. We all know of inhumane traps, but when dealing with a mouse (imagine it is diseased and not just a pest), isn't a mousetrap fitting?[19] And, if we stick with Gregory's universalism, the mousetrap should be imagined as both capturing the mouse *and curing it*. Gregory's image of Jesus as bait for a fish might seem a bit grizzly—the disciples apparently used nets for fishing (Matt 4:18–22)—but in Gregory's ransom theory the bait (Jesus) is killed and yet resurrected while the fish (Satan) is not killed and eaten but redeemed.

The idea that Satan might be overcome or defeated by over-extending his reign, seems to fit in well with what might be called the lessons of history. In pre-Christian times, why did the following empires fall: (in alphabetical order) Assyrian, Athenian, Babylonian, Carthaginian, Egyptian, Hittite, Macedonian or Alexandrian, Persian, Spartan? That might seem like a trick question, for there are many reasons, but I suggest that *over-extension* would be a common thread. I believe over-extension also played

19. Note the mousetrap Hamlet plants to expose the guilt of his stepfather, *Hamlet*, Act III, scene 2.

some role after the life of Christ: witness the end of the Roman and Byzantine empires, Charlemagne's empire, the Mongols, the Azteks, the Spanish and Portuguese empires, Napoleon, the Ottoman empire, Hitler, the British empire. If the Satan hypothesis is alive, the idea that Satan would fall by over-extension would fit into what we learn in world history.

Given the Gregorian ransom theory notion that Satan can be outfoxed (or outwitted), there is some resonance with the role of fairytales enabling their readers to see that evil can indeed be overcome. I cited Chesterton to that effect in chapter one, so here I cite Lewis:

> There is something ludicrous in the idea of so educating a generation which is born to the Ogpu [the secret police in the Soviet Union, 1922–1934] and the atomic bomb. Since it is so likely that they will meet cruel enemies, let them at least have heard of brave knights and heroic courage. . . . I side impenitently with the human race against the modern reformer. Let there be wicked kings and beheadings, battles and dungeons, giants and dragons, and let villains be soundly killed at the end of the book. Nothing will persuade me that this causes an ordinary child any kind or degree of fear beyond what it wants, and needs to feel.[20]

(2) Fairness and the exchange of captives for an innocent person

The ransom is unfair *in the sense that* the innocent person in the thought experiment or Jesus in salvation history did not deserve death. What the kidnappers did and what Satan has done (in the Gregorian ransom theory) should not have happened. But for an innocent person to enter into the fray to liberate captives is a casebook case of heroism and fits in perfectly with Christian tradition. For example, John 15:13: "Greater love has no one than this, that someone lay down his life for his friends." Consider this succinct

20. Hooper, *C. S. Lewis; A Companion & Guide*, 399.

passage from the *Sayings of the Desert Fathers*: "Ab... Agathon said, 'If I could meet a leper, give him my body and ...ke his, I would be very happy.'"[21]

(3) The individual and ancestral guilt

Many of us have strong moral reservations about ho... a person can be guilty of the wrongdoing of ancestors. It appe... that the Gregorian ransom theory holds that our ancestors (e... Adam and Eve or the first wave of homo sapiens) placed u... captivity to Satan. Why should you and I be in such bonda... ransom theology to one side, it is not implausible to think tha... have in fact inherited in the course of our biological evolutio... endency to vice. While not a Christian, the philosopher Micha... Ruse has claimed that the doctrine of original sin receives so... support from Darwinian evolution, according to which our ... interest naturally prompts us to greed and lust.[22] Recent wor... racism has also brought to light how a person can inherit th... nefits of past injustice. A given white person today may have ... ersonal responsibility for past injustice, but he may have inheri... n terms of wealth, property, social advantages, and some good... are the result of ancestral sins and wrongdoing. Arguably, he ... therefore have duties to investigate such past wrongdoings ... er than resort to willful ignorance), to denounce past wrong... restore wealth and property to the descendants of those wro... (if that is possible), and to work for equality of social opportu... With-out taking such measures, the privileged individual ... become morally tainted by past wrongs.[23] So, I am inclined t... ink that the Gregorian ransom theory is not out of tune w... current moral reflection. Each of us alive today may be des... ants of praiseworthy ancestors, but for most of us it is prob... that at least some of our ancestors committed murder, rape, li... harmful

21. In Clement, ed., *The Roots of Christian Mysticism*, 280.

22. Ruse, *Can a Darwinian Be a Christian?*

23. Recent advocates of collective responsibility and guilt ...de Larry May, Peter French, Virginia Held, and D. E. Cooper.

manipulation, exploitation, and so on. This may be likened to our being linked to the demonic.

(4) Sin and Death

In its long history, Christians have diverged on the philosophical theology of death. For many, death came about through the Adamic (original) sin. This has some biblical support; see, for example, the Book of Wisdom 1:12–14:

> Do not bring on your own death by sinful actions. God did not invent death, and when living creatures die, it gives him no pleasure. He created everything so that it might continue to exist, and everything he created is wholesome and good. There is no deadly poison in them. No, death does not rule this world.

But for many Christians and non-Christians today, dying and death seem to be part of our biology. It would seem to many of us miraculous to live 122 years (the age of the oldest living person on record). But the kind of death that is linked with sin in Christian theology is the way in which sin disfigures, poisons, and destroys that which is good. So, when people give themselves over to vain, self-centered values, when parents abuse their children, and when those Japanese soldiers committed war crimes, the heart and soul of vain persons are dead to love and compassion, the parents have ceased to be worthy of being called parents (they have violated or killed their roles of being parents and have instead become enemies of their children and themselves), those soldiers are no longer worthy of being called soldiers but are instead agents who have committed crimes against humanity itself; they are not soldiers, but sadistic terrorists, murderers, rapists deserving the universal and eternal condemnation. Because of their violating the code of war conduct (*jus in bellum*) they have become abominations, a disgrace to their uniform.

In general, Christian theology holds to what may be called *the primacy of the good*. It is held that we, and the created order we are part of, were made for flourishing. Sin and evil are what impede, wrongly use, or manipulate, threaten, and destroy what is good. So, the link between sin and death is direct. When I wrongly treat a student, I have (as it were) killed or destroyed my integrity and have taken what is meant to be a healthy relationship (professor-student relations in higher education) and made myself and that relationship malignant and poisonous. In this framework, vices and wrongdoing are what mortify or deaden our lives. Virtues and right action, especially in the course of atoning love, is instead the source of a life so vital that it does not end with burial and annihilation.

As for physical death itself, from Gregory's point of view, Jesus' life, death, and resurrection has turned physical death into a portal or bridge we must cross in order to enter into an endless, passionate journey toward union with the very fountain of being, the living and life-affirming God. Gregory might add, with C. S. Lewis, "Further up! Further in!"[24]

A Flaw in the Gregorian Ransom Theory

I hope to have convinced you that there is more merit in Gregory's work than meets the eyes of most of his critics. And it needs to be said that if Gregory's theory of atonement is, in the end, unacceptable, he was not alone in his version of the ransom theory. For example, a theologian no less great than Origen of Alexandria makes this independent, free-standing about the ransom of Jesus: "To whom did He [Jesus] pay out his life as a ransom for many? Certainly not to God. Was it then to the evil one? Yes, for it was he who ruled over us, until the life of Jesus was given to the deceiver himself as a ransom for us."[25]

The problem with such theology is that it runs aground on the emphatic Christian teaching that *the body and blood of Christ*

---

24. Lines from *Battle* as the main characters enter Aslan's Country.

25. Origen, *Commentaries on Matthew* in Clement, ed., *The Roots of Christian Mysticism*, 212.

is given for us and offered to us, and that through eating and drinking of the body and blood we may come to new life with the Father.

So, Jesus said to them, "Very truly I will tell you, unless you eat the flesh of the Son of Man and drink his blood, you have no life in you. Those who eat my flesh and drink my blood have eternal life, and I will raise them up on the last day, for my flesh is true food and my blood is true drink. Those who eat my flesh and drink my blood, abide in me and I in them. Just as the Living Father sent me, and I live because of the Father, so whoever eats me will live because of me" (John 6:53–57). There is no hint here or in the other words of Jesus in the Gospels (Luke 22:20; Matt 26:28) that the body and blood of Jesus is actually given to Satan so that Satan might agree to free us from bondage. Instead, *the body and blood of Christ is both given for us and offered to us,* where "us" covers all persons.

It may rightly be asked, if the Gregorian ransom theory has the flaw we have identified, isn't there also a flaw for atonement in Narnia insofar as Aslan gave his life into the hands of the Witch? Maybe so, but note that *putting oneself into the hands of the Witch is not the same thing as giving one's life to or for the Witch.* Aslan gave his life *to* and *for* Edmund and defeated death *through* subjecting himself to the Witch's knife. The killing of Aslan by the Witch was part of *the means by which* the power of sin, death, and of the Witch herself was broken and the Table cracked. So, for all the reasons recounted in chapter one (the Witch's promise to renounce Edmund was not genuine—it was an *illusory promise* or the illusion of a promise, she had no independent standing to kill traitors as she is herself is a traitor, and so on), the Witch was not the recipient of the gifting of Aslan's life. Her killing him was the channel Aslan willingly chose to use to bring life out of death. To appeal to a benign example of letting yourself be subject to another person for a greater purpose rather than giving yourself to someone as a gift or payment, consider going to a surgeon for a major operation. When you go in for surgery you consent for your life (your body and blood) to be subject to the surgeon's knife, but (unless we are to imagine things from a horror-film perspective) you are not giving your life for or to the surgeon. By way of contrast, when you make a wedding vow you are actually giving your life over to another person. The vow would be a conduit, channel, or means by which the marriage comes about, but the marriage itself could be constituted by a mutual self-donation of one person to another. Back to Narnia, *Aslan does not make a self-donation to the Witch, nor does he give her his life as something owed or due to her, something on which she has some kind of claim; rather, the Witch and her killing is the conduit, channel, or means by which Aslan brings about atonement.*

Rejecting the idea that the body and blood was paid to Satan, some theologians altered their version of the ransom theory. A friend of Gregory of Nyssa, St. Gregory the Theologian (also known as Gregory Nazianzus), the fourth-century archbishop of Constantinople, held that the ransom should be understood as the price Christ paid in becoming incarnate. The cost to Jesus in becoming human meant his fully sharing in the human condition, being subject to hunger, suffering, and death. Here is an important passage from his *Second Paschal Oration* in which he asks the question: "To whom was the ransom (Christ's death on the Cross) paid?"

> To Whom was that Blood offered that was shed for us, and why was it shed? I mean the precious and famous Blood of our God and High priest and Sacrifice. We were detained in bondage by the Evil One, sold under sin, and receiving pleasure in exchange for wickedness. Now, since a ransom belongs only to him who holds in bondage, I ask to whom was this offered, and for what cause? If to the Evil One, fie upon the outrage! If the robber receives ransom, not only from God, but a ransom which consists of God Himself, and has such an illustrious payment for his tyranny, a payment for whose sake it would have been right for him to have left us alone altogether. But if to the Father, I ask first, how? For it was not by Him that we were being oppressed; and next, On what principle did the Blood of His Only begotten Son delight the Father, Who would not receive even Isaac,

when he was being offered by his father, but changed the sacrifice, putting a ram in the place of the human victim? Is it not evident that the Father accepts Him, but neither asked for Him nor demanded Him; but on account of the Incarnation, and because Humanity must be sanctified by the Humanity of God, that He might deliver us Himself, and overcome the tyrant, and draw us to Himself by the mediation of His Son, Who also arranged this to the honour of the Father, Whom it is manifest that He obeys in all things? So much we have said of Christ; the greater part of what we might say shall be reverenced with silence.[26]

To distinguish the two Gregorys, I will subsequently use the full titles of each: Gregory of Nyssa and Gregory the Theologian

In the next chapter, let us consider the Christus Victor ransom theory with its focus on different stages of atonement, especially transfiguration and restitution. It involves no bargains or agreements with Satan or the equivalent of the Witch. But it does reflect important elements of atonement found in Narnia.

26. Gregory Nazianzen, *Collection*, chapter XXII, 230–35.

Chapter Three

The Christus Victor
Ransom Theory

As we look to a third ransom theory of the atonement, we do well to note that virtually all Christian theories of the atonement offer a shared vision of the unsurpassable love, beauty, holiness, and superabundant goodness of life at one with God. From a Christian point of view, this is not something that is only postmortem, but something deeply connected with the experience of God, especially through the incarnation, in this life. In one of his Letters to the Corinthians, near the end of the first century, St. Clement writes:

> Who is able to explain the bond of the love of God? No one is equal to the telling of the greatness of His beauty. The height to which love lifts us is unutterable. Love unites us to God. Love covers a multitude of sins. Love endures all things, is long suffering in everything. There is nothing vulgar in love, nothing haughty. Love makes no schism; love does not quarrel; love does everything in unity. In love were all the elect of God perfected; without love nothing is pleasing to God. In love did the Master take hold of us. For the sake of the love which he had for us did Jesus Christ our Lord, by the will of God, give us His blood for us, His flesh for us, and His life for our lives.[1]

1. St. Clement, *Letter to Corinthians*, in Clement, ed., *Roots of Christian*

70

The union with God has been portrayed in Scripture, art, and spiritual tradition using many images: a wedding, the consummation of marriage (in what is called Bridegroom mysticism), a great feast or banquet, a dance, a kiss, a holy city, beatific vision (think of the end of Dante's *Paradiso*), an ecstatic mystical experience (think of Bernini's *The Ecstasy of Saint Teresa* [1647–52] in Rome), gathering by a great fountain, ecstatic worship, and so on. In Narnia, the victory of Aslan is marked in *Lion* first by playing with Susan and Lucy and then, after the defeat of the Witch, by a coronation festival; in *Caspian* victory by Aslan, the children, and the good creatures of Narnia is celebrated by dancing and drinking (with even Bacchus, the god of wine, joining in), and, in *Battle*, by wondrous re-unions, spectacular running and flying, and surprising joy in the midst of an awesome, unending world of mountains, valleys, waterfalls.

So, how do we get there? The Christus Victor ransom theory involves five stages in the course of atonement:

1. sorrowful confession

2. double-movement and moral regeneration

3. forgiveness

4. care and coordination, and

5. transfiguration through restoration.

I propose that this account is at work (with different degrees of emphasis) in the work of St. Gregory the Theologian, St. Irenaeus, and many others. An example of a different degree of emphasis is that Irenaeus places greater stress than Gregory on Christ's saving power in *recapitulating the life of Adam* (reversing Adam's disobedience and imperfection by Christ's obedience and perfection), whereby Christ becomes the New Adam.[2] Still, both saints agree

---

Mysticism, 11. This echoes St. Paul's beautiful hymn to love, 1 Corinthians 13.

2. Irenaeus also gives more attention to Mary recapitulating the life of Eve than Gregory does. He is an exemplar of Christian monks in the medieval era who sought to practice philosophy in the presence of Mary, *philosophari in Maria*. This practice was enjoined by Pope John Paul II in his *Fides Et Ratio*,

that Christ defeats sin, death, and the devil, and they agree on the importance of confession, repentance, renewal, forgiveness, and our transfiguration into the life of God as God restores and heals creation. In presenting the Christus Victor ransom theory in this chapter, I use terms like "double-movement" and "bare forgiveness" that you will not find in work by Gregory, Irenaeus, and others, but my aim is *not* to introduce my own original ideas but to find ways for us all to engage this promising account of atonement.[3]

One more, brief preparatory note: Gregory the Theologian, Irenaeus, and others in this tradition contended that Christ's incarnation hallowed the different stages of our lives. They were keenly aware that for most of us atonement rarely happens all at once or in only one stage of our lives. Most persons may pass many stages of life in finding our way into God's presence. In *Against Heresies* Irenaeus writes:

> He came to save all through Himself—all, I say, who through Him are reborn in God—infants and children, and youth and old men. Therefore, He passed through every age, becoming an infant for infants, sanctifying infants, sanctifying those who are of that age, and at the same time becoming for them an example of piety, of righteousness, and submission; a young man for youths, becoming an example for youth and sanctifying them in the Lord. So also He became an old man for old men so that He might be the perfect teacher in all things—perfect not only in respect to the setting forth of truth, but perfect in respect to relative age—sanctifying the elderly and at the same time becoming an example to them. Then He even experienced death itself, so that He might be the firstborn from the dead, having the first place in

---

in which he urged people to practice philosophizing *with Mary.* I suggest this means (in part) that we are to be receptive to what God may reveal; in the words of the Angelis, "Be it unto me, according to Thy word."

3. This chapter reflects the work of Paul Reasoner (to whom this book is dedicated) and myself in a paper "The Double-Movement in Buddhist and Christian Rituals."

all things, the originator of life before all and preceding all.[4]

Let us now turn to the different stages in the Christus Victor ransom theory.

The Five Stages in the Christus Victor Ransom Theory

I present the stages in the context of what philosophers call a thought experiment. Imagine you and I are in a relationship—we are either married or co-workers or friends—and I wrong you. Let's imagine three wrongs with increased gravity: I steal from you something of modest value (your fountain pen); I betray you in a serious fashion—if we are married, I am unfaithful; if we are colleagues, I report (falsely) that you have committed some infraction that places your professional life in danger. Even more grave, I have assaulted you or, still more grave, I have either killed you or your child. What, if anything, might be done for there to be an atonement between us? I suggest that five stages would (ideally) need to take place: a sorrowful confession in which I renounce the wrong; a double-movement involving repentance and moral regeneration; forgiveness; our mutual acknowledgement of our shared acts; and transfiguration through restitution. I consider each stage with some comments on the nuances involved. As should be obvious, the possibility of atonement between us is especially problematic in human terms if I have killed you, though matters change in the context of the Christus Victor ransom theory.

1. Sorrowful Confession

It is not enough for me to confess my wrong to God or to the church. Ideally, it must be *to you*. A voluntary confession has greater merit (or less demerit) than one that is forced. This is because confession

---

4. Irenaeus, *Against Heretics* in Clement, ed., *The Roots of Christian Mysticism*, 87.

needs to involve my repudiation of the wrong. It must be sorrowful, as this displays or embodies my renunciation of the act. If I still take pleasure in what I have done, then I have failed to repudiate the wrong. Repudiation also confirms that not only do I regret the act and its outcome, I have remorse.

Some further qualifications: (a) I suggest that a conditional confession may be suspect—*"If I offended you,* I am sorry" hints at a failure to own up to a wrong. (b) Sometimes confession to the wrongdoer is not possible. If I have killed you, then short of an afterlife, confessing to you is obviously impossible. (c) Confession to your family or to your community or society at large may be important, secondary factors. (d) For Christians (and most religious theists) confession to God is vital.

On the point (d) we may pause to consider an objection. Being omniscient, God already knows my every wrong (sin). What is the point of confession in that context?

A reply: In chapter one, I stressed the good of participation in relation to Aslan. In our world there is the good of participating in relationship with our Aslan, God, living *Coram Deo* (in the presence of God). When we sin, we rupture that relationship. In some Christian traditions that rupture can be profoundly damaging (mortal sin) or a less grave matter (venial sin) in which one's life *Coram Deum* is not severed but tarnished.[5] Confession in private prayer or auricular confession (confession in the presence of a priest) or a general confession (as in most rites of the Eucharist or Holy Communion) is a way of ritually owning one's wrong. Because we are embodied beings, there is an enormous significance on how and when we embody or physically manifest our values, whether this is through only oral confession or, in an enhanced rite, we embody our confession with contrite kneeling. Yes, God does not need to hear my confession to know my sin and the sincerity of my repudiation, but the confession is not intended to pass new information on to God. Rather, in the course of my relationship with God there is an irreplaceable role in physically displaying my repudiation of my sin through an intentional act to

5. See Mellema, *Sin*, chapter 4, "Mortal and Venial Sin."

God, to myself, and perhaps to my church and community as well. It is because of the importance of physically manifesting contrition, that much of Christian spiritual literature includes a kind of guide to weeping and tears.[6] Confession is one stage among others to welcome renewed (repaired or redeemed) participation of a life lived in the presence of God.[7]

2. Double-Movement of Repentance and Moral Regeneration

I propose that for there to be an atonement between me and you, I need to identify myself as the person who truly wronged you and yet, through repentance, forming new desires and dispositions to not harm you again. Double-movement means moving to the past while moving to the future. (Double-movement needs to be distinguished from what may be called self-separation. The later involves a case of when the wrongdoer so renounces their past wrong that they regard themselves as a completely different person. Self-separation is if I claimed that it was not me that harmed you, but Charles, whereas I am Charlie—giving myself a new name, to mark my regeneration.)

The double-movement stage amounts to a spiritual and moral re-generation. This re-generation may be pictured with an image of the Greek mythic bird, the Phoenix. In the book *The Ultimate Harry Potter and Philosophy: Hogwarts for Muggles*, I advocate the double-movement model in the context of J. K. Rowling's Harry Potter books, especially *The Deathly Hallows*.[8] I liken the double-movement account as a kind of dying to one's old self, and rising to a new identity, as one finds in the case of Harry, Professor

6. See, for example, John Climacus, *The Ladder of Divine Ascent*. There are many cases of crying in the Bible; in terms of contrition, the most famous may be Peter's bitter crying when he betrays Jesus three times (Luke 22:62).

7. For a philosophy of religious rites, see Taliaferro, "Religious Rites."

8. Taliaferro, "The Real Secret of the Phoenix: Moral Regeneration though Death." Spiritual and moral regeneration plays an important part in much of the New Testament, e.g., Col 3:1–17 urges us to kill in ourselves wrong desires and to put on a new self. Interestingly, St. Clement likened Christ to the phoenix in his Letter to the Corinthians.

Dumbledore, and Severus Snape. It is because Tom Riddle (aka Voldemort) cannot engage in the essential remorse, repudiation of the past, and repentance that he becomes, in the end, completely undone.

3. Forgiveness

The definition of forgiveness is subject to some dispute. In modern thought, forgiveness has customarily been analyzed as the moderation or repudiation of resentment. You forgive me when you moderate or perhaps even repudiate your resentment of me. I have reservations about this model for two reasons.

First, you may lessen your resentment of me, not because you forgive me, but because you simply hate being resentful. Or perhaps over the years you might forget my wrongdoing and thus have no resentment, but this would not be the same as forgiving me.

Second, "resentment," at least in English, seems very close to a vice or something undesirable, like smoldering hatred. If we believe God forgives us, do we have to believe that God must be subject to resentment, even if God may repudiate such resentment? That seems odd, though maybe if we re-interpreted forgiveness as a setting aside of *anger*, it may be more plausible in a biblical context (e.g., Isa 5:25). But it seems we can easily recognize genuine cases of forgiveness—especially between healthy parents and their children—when no anger or resentment is at issue at all.

I suggest we think of forgiveness in terms of *deliberately ceasing to blame the one who is forgiven*. This does not mean denying the wrong act nor even claiming that the one who is forgiven should be pardoned or released from punishment. Perhaps I need to be punished for my wrong as a means for my reformation (my double-movement) or the punishment needs to take place to communicate to society that acts like mine are intolerable. Isaac of Nineveh, a great Syrian monk in the seventh century, rightly identifies any punishment, from a Christian point of view, as loving: "God in his love punishes, not to take revenge, far from it. He seeks the restoration of his own image."[9] Setting aside punishment for the moment, I propose that once you have forgiven me, you would not continue a daily practice of blaming me for the past act, e.g., "Charles, do you remember your betrayal of me last summer? You are a pathetic waste of time and space!"

However you define forgiveness, I suggest there are two types of forgiveness, what we may call *bare forgiveness* and *reconciliatory forgiveness*.

Consider first *reconciliatory forgiveness*. If you and I are truly to be reconciled or for there to be atonement, then I propose that I must undertake a credible confession, the double-movement, and regeneration. For us to resume our relationship under conditions when I believe I have not harmed you in any way would seem to make you vulnerable to further harm and perhaps other ills like humiliation, shame, and grief. However, if there is no relationship to resume (and no new relationship to forge), then it seems to me that that forgiveness might still take place insofar as you cease the practice of blaming me or (if you accept the traditional definition of forgiveness) you moderate or renounce your resentment or anger toward me. This latter is what I call *bare forgiveness*.

Though not essential to the overall portrait of atonement developed here, I offer three further observations for your consideration.

First, I propose that forgiveness is rarely a matter of moral obligation. If I have wronged you, then (*ceteris paribus*) I think it is "up to you" whether you forgive me or not. We can think of some cases where we might feel bound to forgive (we live together in a monastery and have made vows to forgive one another or in the context of a healthy parent-child relationship), but I suggest it is rare among adults that this is the norm. (One caveat: the line in the Lord's Prayer—"forgive us our trespasses, as we forgive those who trespass against us"—sets up a kind of reciprocity with God. In offering this prayer, you are not [ipso facto] obligated to forgive others, but you are linking your practicing forgiveness of others

9. Isaac of Nineveh, *Ascetic Treatises*, in Clement, ed., *The Roots of Christian Mysticism*, 299.

to God's forgiving you. If you do not forgive another person's trespass, you risk being unforgiven for your trespasses.)

Second, I suggest that forgiveness may take time. It may take hours, weeks, maybe years for you to forgive me. On either definition of forgiveness, it may take time to renounce anger or resentment or to cease blaming a wrongdoer. You may well overtly cease such blaming and yet you might still resolutely harbor such blame.

Third, although I am not singling out self-forgiveness as a distinct stage in atonement, I believe it is essential in reconciliatory forgiveness. Arguably, it has to have a role in the double-movement and regeneration. Arguably, I will not be able to engage in moral and spiritual regeneration if I am locked into continual blaming of myself for my past wrong.

4. Care and Coordination

Ideally, the interaction between you and me needs to be clear and faithful. Obviously, there still might be atonement amidst confusion and partial, non-ideal conditions, but a great deal of Christian spiritual literature urges us to aim at a life-affirming, respectful, even loving atonement. Consider the following passage from the twelfth-century classic *Spiritual Friendship* by St. Aelred of Rievaulx. Aelred is particularly concerned about how two friends might repair their relationship after an infraction.

> For I have seen some, in correcting their friends, clothe with the name of zeal, now of liberty, the bitterness within them and their outsurging rage; and because they follow impulse rather than reason, they never effect any good by such corrections but rather cause harm. But among friends there is no reason for this vice. For a friend ought to sympathize with a friend, he ought to . . . think of his friend's fault as his own, to correct him humbly and sympathetically. Let a somewhat troubled countenance make the reproof, as also a saddened utterance; let tears interrupt words, so that the other may not

only see but even feel that the reproof proceeds from love rather than rancor.[10]

Ever the student of loving intimacy, Aelred recognizes that there is an art to reconciliation.

Because this stage of what I am calling care and coordination is often neglected in the literature on atonement, I cite one more passage akin to Aelred's on the art of reconciliation. In the seventh century, Maximus the Confessor offered a detailed guide to reconciliation:

> Has your brother been an occasion of trial for you? Has your annoyance led you to hatred? Do not let yourself be defeated, but triumph over hatred by love. This is the way to do it: by praying to God sincerely for him; by accepting the excuses others make for him or by constituting yourself his defender; by taking responsibility for your trial on yourself and bearing it with courage until the cloud has lifted.
>
> Be careful, if you were praising the goodness and proclaiming the virtue of someone yesterday, not to disparage him today as wicked and perverse, just because your affection has turned to aversion. Do not seek by blaming your brother to justify your culpable aversion but continue faithfully praising him, even if you are overcome with annoyance, and you will soon return to a wholesome charity. . . . The whole purpose of our Lord's commandments is to rescue the spirit from chaos and hatred and lead it to love of him and love of one's neighbor. From this springs forth, like a flash of lightning, holy knowledge.[11]

I highly commend his dexterous wisdom, forged by many years in monasteries, when living together was sometimes badly in need of holy knowledge.

---

10. Aelred of Rievaulx, *Spiritual Friendship*, 121.

11. Maximus the Confessor, *Centuries on Charity* in Clement, ed., *The Roots of Christian Mysticism*, 277.

5. Transfiguration through Restitution

We now come to an important intersection of human and divine activity. In the cases I have proposed in mapping a model of atonement, restitution is straightforward only with a minor infraction such as the stealing of your pen. Of course, this event might be momentous (the pen was gifted to you by a dying parent, and the theft by me was intended to be malicious), but under ordinary conditions getting you a new pen or perhaps a dozen new pens (plus enviable Italian stationary and a leather pen carrier) might be a proper restitution. Matters escalate with betrayal. In the case of my betraying you in a professional context, perhaps my confession, double-movement, and regeneration might be paired with my arranging for you to be promoted to a highly desirable rank with a massive salary increase plus stock options. But in the case of betrayal in a marriage or deep friendship, matters are deeply confounding. How can I give you back the twelve years we have been married or been friends? And, of course, in the case of when I have killed your child or you, the very idea of restitution seems preposterous.

Maybe so. Most theists in all religious and philosophical traditions hold that even God cannot change the past; if I killed your child last year, even God cannot alter that fact. Even so, in Christian tradition (as well as in many theistic religious traditions) God can ensure that biological death is not the complete annihilation of persons. Indeed, the good news in the Christian Gospels and throughout the New Testament is that Jesus Christ has overcome death, sin, and the devil.

Christians have differed in their treatment of death and the afterlife. Placing to one side those who treat as only metaphors or myths the resurrection narratives and claims about everlasting life, most Christians have believed that at death you (or your soul) is either *Coram Deo* (in the presence of God) or alienated from God, while some claim that one only comes into God's presence or experiences a hellish afterlife at the resurrection of one's body. There are also hybrid views to the effect that while the resurrection of your body will mark your fully restored (transformed) identity, there is an "intermediate state" between your death and resurrection in which you are "asleep with the Lord" or enjoy some relationship with God.

The view that at death we are in the presence of God is often supported biblically by 2 Cor 5:1–10. Commenting on this passage, Thomas Aquinas writes: "*Therefore, the answer is that* the saints see the essence of God immediately after death and dwell in a heavenly mansion. Thus, therefore, it is plain that the reward which saints await is inestimable." Thomas Aquinas, *Commentary on the Letters of Saint Paul to the Corinthians*, 472. Other biblical elements that are appealed to in support of the view that persons endure an immediate life after death (rather than waiting for the physical resurrection of their bodies) include the appearance of Moses and Elijah in the transfiguration (Matt 17:1–9), the descent into hell, where Jesus seeks out persons whose bodies have not been resurrected (1 Pet 4:6), the parable of the rich man and Lazarus (Luke 16:19–31). The idea that persons at death are immediately with God is supported by the practice of praying for those who have died and invoking saints (including Mary) to pray on our behalf

Part of the intuitive force behind the idea that persons are no longer present after biological death lies in our reluctance to think of the dead person still existing *as their body* after death. Most of us think of the dead body as a corpse or refer to it as a person's remains.

In this book, I adopt C. S. Lewis' Narnian perspective in which death (as portrayed in *Battle*) marks the point at which there is a radical transformation and persons are re-embodied and able to interact in recognizable ways in a realm other than this world. Like Lewis, I am in the Christian Platonist tradition, holding that persons (and perhaps some nonhuman animals) are not entirely or solely physical organisms; there is more to your conscious, subjective identity than your physical anatomy and neurological

processes.[12] Materialist treatments of persons have bee   ubject to
serious criticism by a host of philosophers today.[13]

From a Christian, theistic point of view, we have s   reason
to hope for life after this life if we are able (or at lea   not treat
with routine contempt) to envisage the possibility that   destruction of one's body is not (ipso facto) the irreversible de   ction of
you.[14] In the Christian tradition, God is understood to   created
persons. Because such love is fundamentally benefi   d (desir-
ous of the good of the beloved), if the flourishing of   ons can
unfold in a life beyond this life as a greater and great   ena for
atonement and love, such a realm beyond this life seem   though
it would be very much part of God's bounteous, ov   elming
love. And if Gregory of Nyssa is right that God's omn   ent love
is limitless, the ending of this life may mark the begi   g of an
ever-expanding life on into eternity. Note that this lo   g for life
beyond this life is not grounded in any selfish or nar   istic perspective. It is grounded in the longing for a transcend   good for
all or at least for all who choose to seek it out.

Before further exploring how new life might c   ibute to
restitution, let's pause to consider when a life beyond th   e would
fail to embody great goods or personal transformatio   If the afterlife is akin to the land of shadows portrayed in Hom   c poetry
(especially the *Iliad*) and in the early Hebrew notio   *eol* (the
abode of the dead), then "life" after death would seem   a stag-
nant, bloodless place of despair. Things don't look mu   etter in
Dante's *Inferno* where characters seem to be trapped i   ir vices.

12. For an overview of Christian Platonism see Hampton an   nny, eds.,
Christian Platonism: A History.

13. Contemporary critics of materialism include Mark Bak   hua Far-
ris, John Foster, Stewart Goetz, E. J. Lowe, William Hasker,   t Koons,
Jonathan Loose, David Lund, J. P. Moreland, Thomas Nagel, A   Menuge,
Howard Robinson, T. L. S. Sprigge, Richard Swinburne, Char   iliaferro,
Dean Zimmerman.

14. See my entry "Afterlife" in the free and online *Stanfor   clopedia
of Philosophy.* For an excellent response to theologians who disp   the traditional belief in the soul, see Goetz, "Is N.T. Wright ab   ubstance
Dualism?"

If we imagine an afterlife along the lines of Sartre's 1944 play *No Exit*, then it looks like hell. If we imagine it as a mere extension of the pleasures and pains of this life, it seems that an afterlife would involve no more goods or ills than we currently face. Adding other pleasures, even super-pleasures like being able to fly or engage in new sensual delights, seems destined to become fallow after a few thousand years. Moreover, what may be called *bare restitution* would seem neither atoning nor transforming for any of us. If I have ruined our friendship, and you and I are given life beyond life, I might ruin it again. And just how might my ruining a marriage with you be restored? Would we be given a new apartment by a great fountain to try again? Even worse, if you or your child are brought back to life, maybe I might re-enact my earlier act.

Such reflection yields the conclusion that any concept of life beyond life that is atoning must be seen as an arena of transformation by God, envisaged by Gregory of Nyssa, Origen, Isaac of Nineveh, Dionysius, and others as an ocean of life-giving love and transformation. What is key is that in that transformation, wrongdoers such as me must come to identify with the work of re-creation by Jesus Christ. Consider, for instance, Romans 6:5–7:

> For if we have been united with him in a death like his, we will certainly be united with him in a resurrection like his. We know that our old self was crucified with him so that the body of sin might be destroyed, and we might no longer be enslaved to sin. For whoever has died is freed from sin.

In Colossians 3:1–17 there is an explicit identification of Christ as your life:

> If then you have been raised with Christ, seek the things that are above, where Christ is, seated at the right hand of God. Set your minds on things that are above, not on things that are on earth. For you have died, and your life is hidden with Christ in God. When Christ *who is your life* [emphasis mine] appears, then you also will appear with him in glory.

> Put to death therefore what is earthly in you: sexual immorality, impurity, passion, evil desire, and covetousness, which is idolatry. On account of these the wrath of God is coming. In these you too once walked, when you were living in them. But now you must put them all away: anger, wrath, malice, slander, and obscene talk from your mouth. Do not lie to one another, seeing that you have put off the old self with its practices and have put on the new self, which is being renewed in knowledge after the image of its creator. Here there is not Greek and Jew, circumcised and uncircumcised, barbarian, Scythian, slave, free; but Christ is all, and in all.

What might it mean for Christ to be your life? For one, it means your identity is not solely or merely a matter of your ethnicity, tribal origin, and so on. If Christ is your life it means you must be one with Christ in willing the fruits of his resurrection as the promise to heal and restore that which has been harmed or destroyed. This would involve a transfiguration by which you become united with Christ.

What would divine restitution and repair of past harms and destruction look like? In the case of my killing you or your child, renewed life beyond death would provide an arena for the transfiguration of our lives, putting to death malice and other vices, and participating together in God's redemptive love. Restitution and restoration may be straightforward in simple cases, such as the case of restoring an ear in Luke chapter 22. During the betrayal and arrest of Jesus, someone strikes the servant of the high priest, cutting off his ear. "Jesus touched the man's ear and healed him" (v. 51). But restitution and restoration of so many things—from malignant horrors, like torturing another person, to grave but lesser matters, like personal betrayal—are deeply disturbing.

We are perhaps able to see cases of how, in this life, the experience of God's loving compassion may transform or transfigure persons. This seems to be the case in many of the lives recorded in Christian tradition, beginning with the early disciples. Peter betrays Jesus three times, but he is eventually transformed to become one of the leading apostles to unify the early church in its teaching, welcoming gentiles. Paul persecuted the early Christ-followers, even approving the violent execution of Stephen, but then he was turned around and renewed as the most important of the apostles to spread (or initiate the spreading) of the good news of Jesus throughout the Roman Empire. Examples of saints whose early lives were profligate or distorted can be amply multiplied—Augustine, Francis, Ignatius, Dorothy Day, and so on—but who found unity or atonement with God in lives of serving others for the love of God. Perhaps the best-known Christian hymn today is "Amazing Grace"; it was authored by John Newton, one-time captain of slave ships, after he converted to Christianity and eventually become an abolitionist. It has come to represent his radical transformation from participating in the slave trade to opposing it.

As for how an afterlife may be conceived in which there is a transforming atonement between persons and with God, some literature may be helpful. Shakespeare wrote plays in which there are apparent deaths and then life-enhancing re-unions between partners who were in strife. His *Cymbeline* and *The Winter's Tale* offer us some guidance to reconciliation. In the latter, King Leontis believes he is responsible for his wife Hermione's death. He repents and laments for many years. It turns out, however, that she is not dead. The King is presented with what appears to be a statue of Hermione. And it becomes clear that the apparent statue is really the Queen herself. Paulina, the daughter of Leontis and Hermione declares:

> Music, awake her: strike!—[*music*].
> 'Tis time; descend; be stone no more; approach;
> Strike all that look upon with marvel. Come;
> I'll fill your grace up: stir; nay, come away;
> Bequeath to death your numbness, for from him
> Dear life redeems you.—You perceive she stirs:
> [HERMIONE *comes down from the pedestal.*]
> Start not; her actions shall be holy as
> You hear my spell is lawful: do not shun her
> Until you see her die again; for then
> You kill her double. Nay, present your hand:
> When she was young you woo'd her; now in age

Is she become the suitor.

(*Winter's Tale*, Act V, scene III)

The ending speaks to the recovery of romantic love. This is not a tale of an actual afterlife, but a portrait of restoration after a presumed death. Nonetheless, it may offer us helpful insight.

More *directly* relevant are texts such as the following:

- Dante's *Purgatorio* and *Paradiso*, tracing the upward journey of the soul, is rich with imaginative insight.

- C. S. Lewis provides a suggestive picture of heaven and hell in his 1946 book, *The Great Divorce*.

- Evelyn Underhill's novel *The Greyworld* narrates the soul of a boy who has died.

- Almost all the novels of Charles Williams (a close friend of Lewis) give us a view of reality in which the border between this world and the next is porous, especially in *Ash Wednesday* and *Descent into Hell*.

- Philosopher Peter Kreeft has written a series of books in which Socrates questions great philosophers after they have died. Perhaps the most interesting for current readers is *Between Heaven and Hell: A Dialogue Somewhere beyond Death with John F. Kennedy, C. S. Lewis, and Aldous Huxley*. Kennedy, Lewis, and Huxley died on the same day, November 22, 1963. Kreeft imagines what a dialogue between them might look like after they died.

So, novels, poetry, films, songs, paintings, and dances can stir up in us some dim notion of the redeeming possibilities of an afterlife, as envisaged in the Christian tradition.[15] I find inspiring how

---

15. See especially George MacDonald's *Lilith*, which pictures postmortem reconciliation and transformation. Theologically speaking, the theology of an ongoing redemptive journey after death is grounded in Origen's eschatology (which is in turn grounded in earlier theological ideas) and was especially popular among certain nineteenth-century British theologians. On Origen, see Ramelli, *A Larger Hope, Vol. 1*; on the nineteenth century, see Parry, *A Larger Hope? Vol 2*.

many Eastern Orthodox theologians sketch the afterlife in terms of overwhelming love. The great Syrian mystic Isaac of Nineveh even describes hell as a state in which souls feel divine love, but because they elect not to accept and return the love of God and of other creatures, it may feel painful:

> As for me, I say that those who are tormented in hell are tormented by the invasion of love. What is there more bitter and more violent than the pains of love? Those who feel that they have sinned against love bear in themselves a damnation much heavier than the most dreaded punishments. . . . It is absurd to suppose that sinners in hell are deprived of God's love. Love . . . is offered impartially. But by its very power it acts in two ways. It torments sinners, as happens here on earth when we are tormented by the presence of a friend to whom we have been unfaithful. And it gives joy to those who have been faithful.[16]

Isaac goes on to claim that God's almighty loving compassion will ultimately overcome human wickedness:

> As is a grain of sand weighed against a large amount of gold, so, in God, is the demand for equitable judgment weighed against his compassion. As a handful of sand in the boundless ocean, so are the sins of the flesh in comparison with God's providence and mercy. As a copious spring could not be stopped with a handful of dust, so the Creator's compassion cannot be conquered by the wickedness of creatures.[17]

If we cannot have a clear account of just how transfiguration through restoration would (or will) work, is that a problem for the

---

In my view, reports of near-death experiences (including reports of out-of-body experiences) are more impressive than recognized by contemporary philosophers. See Miller, *Near-Death Experiences*. He has assembled hundreds of accounts, many of which provide different narratives of what may lie beyond death.

16. Isaac of Nineveh, *Ascetic Treatises* in Clement, ed., *The Roots of Christian Mysticism*, 303.

17. Isaac of Nineveh, *Ascetic Treatises* in Clement, ed., *The Roots of Christian Mysticism*, 306.

Christus Victor ransom theory? I don't think so. Christian tradition itself affirms that envisaging future states about being in the presence of God surpass human experience. Witness Paul, quoting Isaiah 64:4:

> However, as it is written:
> "What no eye has seen, nor ear heard,
> nor the heart of man imagined,
> what God has prepared for those who love him."
> (1 Cor 2:9)

I suggest it might be quite odd if we could out exactly how life beyond this life might usher in greater and greater levels of atonement. The philosopher Jerry Walls, who has studied and written on heaven and hell extensively, offers this general observation about the alluring nature of the dream of heaven:

> Whatever we believe about the matter, once the reality of heaven has invaded our hearts and stirred our imagination and hopes, it is hard, if not impossible, to recoil from it without a shattering sense of disappointment. Heaven holds out the hope that our deepest longings for fulfillment and happiness can be satisfied not only for a period, but forever. To discard this dream and embrace a timely death as the best we can do is not merely a prudential compromise, but a profound surrender of hope. Only the reality of heaven can prevent our lives from ending with such a whimper.[18]

Further Objections and Replies

Some objections to the ransom theory have been addressed earlier in this chapter and in chapters one and two, concerning individuals and ancestral wrongs, for example, or the charge that it would be better just to bring life out of death without the suffering, death, and resurrection of Aslan/Christ. Consider four other objections.

---

18. Walls, "Heaven and Hell," 251.

First objection: Doesn't the Christus Victor ransom theory wind up distorting our understanding of the gravity of sin and death? If I kill you and yet you are still in being or will be resurrected, does that not lessen the gravity of my crime? If most or all the ill effects of sin and wrongdoing might be (or will be) reversed (enabling restoration, as Origen would put it), aren't our efforts to injure or help each other rendered fatuous?

Reply: If I knew with certainty that the Christus Victor ransom theory was correct, then I would know that my effort to annihilate you would be unsuccessful, for I would then know that the God of omnipotent love would move to redeem your life. Actually, if I did possess such knowledge, it is hard for me to imagine thinking I could get away with any wrongdoing of any kind. But few claim to know with certainty (that is, with knowledge that is infallible and incorrigible) the truth of Christianity. While there are some who claim to know with certainty the falsehood of Christianity (Galen Strawson), absolute claims to know its falsity are rare (even the skeptic Bertrand Russell called himself an agnostic rather than an atheist, for he felt he could not rule out the existence of God). In a case of when we do not know for sure whether or not the God of Christianity will seek our atonement, our wrongdoing and morally courageous acts are just as horrifying or beautiful as they appear to be.

A distinction may be called for between *existential goods and ills* versus what might be called *eschatological or eternal goods and ills*. From an existential vantage point, the evil of a murder in this life is a grave, irrevocable, intolerable wrong. The wrongness of the act is not altered by anything that comes afterwards. If the Christus Victor ransom theory is right, the evil of the murder is not at all removed; the murderer committed a vile act. And yet, from the standpoint of the Christus Victor theory, because there is a resurrection and opportunity for transformation, then, while there is no less evil in the murderous act, there is an occasion for redemption in another passage of life in which death does not have the last word.

Furthermore, if it turns out that the Christus Victor ransom theory is true, then the disvalue or value of our harming or helping each other is *magnified*. When I injure you, I am not only harming a valuable being, which is bad enough, I am also failing to participate in God's holy will for you and creation. When I help others, on the other hand, I am not only helping you, I am also acting in accord with God's holy purpose for creation.

Second objection: While the Christus Victor ransom theory is not necessarily committed to the view that all creatures will, in the end, find atonement with God (as affirmed by Gregory of Nyssa and Origen of Alexandria), it is sympathetic to it. Yet doesn't that form of universalism undermine free will? If we truly have significant freedom that is honored by God, shouldn't we retain the freedom to reject God?

Reply: Maybe so. Maybe not. As my aim is to promote the Christus Victor theory to as many readers as possible, I am presenting it with as few conditions as possible. Thus, you might side with Gregory of Nyssa and his contemporary defenders, maintaining that human freedom is fully compatible with the final redemption of all creatures. Alternatively, you might argue, as C. S. Lewis did, that God cannot *guarantee* that free creatures will be redeemed because human freedom could forever be resisted.[19]

A cutting-edge controversy today, especially among evangelical-leaning Christians who are not universalists, is over whether hell (life apart from God) is everlasting. The view that it will be everlasting until persons abandon sin and seek God has been supported with reference to Dante's *Inferno*, even though Dante himself did not believe that hell might be escaped. On the gates of hell is a sign: "Abandon Hope All Ye Who Enter Here." Arguably all those in Dante's hell are still in the grip of their sinful desires. For instance, the lovers, Paolo and Franscesca, are blown by the wind and still wrapped up in their adultery. It has been suggested that

19. As noted earlier, although some advocates of the ransom theory, like Origin and Gregory of Nyssa, are universalists, believing that all persons will be redeemed is not essential to the Christus Victor ransom theory. One may hold that salvation is universally offered, but not universally accepted by all persons.

they might be released from their domain of hell if they abandoned their disordered passion. As I am presenting it, the Christus Victor ransom theory does not take sides on that matter; the theory might even be accepted by those who believe that God will permit the annihilation of creatures who choose such an end.

Two further, brief observations. First, I suggest that most advocates of the Christus Victor theory believe that God's ransom is offered to *all* creatures. In other words, the view called "limited atonement"— which claims that Christ only died for a subset of humanity, namely, those whom God had chosen from eternity to save (i.e., the elect)—seems out of keeping with the spirit of the Christus Victor perspective. From the Christus Victor point of view, all persons have been created to return to God (be atoned) through Christ. Maximus the Confessor offers this sweeping vision about how the incarnation lovingly summons us to experience God as Christ. Perhaps not all creatures will respond to this invitation, nonetheless, the invitation goes out to the whole world:

> Christ is the great hidden mystery, the blessed goal, the purpose for which everything was created. . . . With his gaze fixed on this goal God called things into existence. He [Christ] is the point to which Providence is tending, together with everything in its keeping, and at which creatures accomplish their return to God.[20]

Second, in the context of reflecting on the afterlife, we do well to recognize that for many Christians "heaven" and "hell" (and perhaps also purgatory, if such a realm exists) begins here and now and not only some future state.[21] This is reflected in the Gospel of John when eternal life is depicted as present as well as in the future (John 5:24; 17:3; see also 1 John 5:2–13). In Marlowe's *Faustus* the demon Mephistopheles tells Faustus that while he, Mephistopheles, is with him he is not out of hell. Hell can begin here and now.

Third objection: Exactly how might restoration impact atonement? You have conceded that bare restoration may be

20. Maximus the Confessor, *Questions to Thalassius* in Clement, ed., *The Roots of Christian Mysticism*, 39.

21. For a defense of purgatory, see Walls, *Purgatory*.

useless, e.g., if someone you killed is resurrected you might just try to kill them again. But even in a case where there is some success and (for example) someone you have killed has been raised from the dead by Christ and you rejoice in this miracle, how can such a restoration by Christ be atoning *for you*? After all, you did not raise the person from the dead. Imagine you are driving recklessly and cause a traffic accident; you hit a car and the other driver and passengers are dying. A driver pulls up and heals the injuries. To make the case quasi-religious, imagine the stranger gives their own blood to heal the injured. Granted that the stranger has altered the ethical and legal predicament: thanks to the stranger, you did not kill others. But that does not seem to be something you can take credit for. And we do not get any more illumination on this if we alter the thought experiment and imagine that the rescuer is no stranger but a close friend of yours or your spouse or sibling or parent.

Reply: Excellent objection! It bring to light the fact that the Christus Victor ransom theory only works if the restitution takes place with *the transfiguration of the wrongdoer*. This is no mere transition in which a person turns from vice to virtue. This transfiguration has to do with the process described at the end of chapter two, when we noted how feeding and drinking the body and blood of Christ are ways to become one with Christ and then one with the Father. The transfiguration is a matter of the wrong-doer becoming one with the rescuer. This oneness is closer and more transcendent than the relations described in the thought experiment: being a stranger, close friend, spouse, sibling, parent. Consider Galatians 2:20 where Paul writes: "I have been crucified with Christ and I no longer live, but Christ lives in me. The life I now live in the body, I live by faith in the Son of God, who loved me and gave himself for me."

To move the thought experiment closer to what is envisaged in the Christus Victor ransom theory, some of the details need to be adjusted. I know the thought-experiment will seem to boarder on the comic or ridiculous, but then I fully admit that the Christus

Victor ransom theory involves elements that extravagantly go beyond ordinary life and our everyday expectations.

Imagine, again, I cause an accident by my reckless driving and the people in the other car are dying. A rescuer named Chris and assistant named Paraclete show up. Chris not only heals and restores those injured of their physical wounds but works deeply to provide healing to them for their own past wrongdoing and those they have harmed. Chris offers saving healing also to me and restores to life and healing all others who have suffered from my past wrongs and provides healing to all the first responders (police, medics, firefighters), and all bystanders. Chris then calls us all to form a common bond of love for each other in which we treat each one's well-being with the same intensity as we treat our own. We are called upon to rejoice in the redeemed healing. The assistant, Paraclete, then (as Aslan does in Narnia) breathes on each of us and we are swept up into a dance, not unlike the celebration at the end of *Caspian*. Chris and Paraclete invite us all to join them in a journey to someone they call "the Father." Arguably, I may still need to be arrested (or fined) for reckless driving; the healing and transfiguration does not change the fact that I caused what would have been the death of others, were it not for Chris. But, thanks to Chris, *the meaning of what took place has changed.* What would have been a plain and simple tragic case of vehicular homicide became the occasion of a joyful celebration for the deliverance of us all from various evils and the establishment of what might be a life-long relationship with each other and a mysterious trinity of Chris, Paraclete, and the Father.

The objector may persist: Even if I grant that your thought experiment is successful in replying to my initial objection, there is what might be called the problem of time. Let it be granted that the restoring work of Jesus is precisely as envisaged by advocates of the Christus Victor ransom account. Still, at the time of Christ's birth, life, teaching, suffering, death, and resurrection, you and I were not "one with Christ." It is Christ, through the power of the Father and Holy Spirit, who promises restoration; any claim that we might participate in this restitution is after the fact (*ex post facto*). Christ may act as our representative, but he ... prior to our choosing to follow him and certainly before w... are born. In that case, how can the power and effects of his p... work be appropriated by us today?

In response I suggest that this is not at all myster... Think of the negative ways we can appropriate past wrongdo... If I persist in enjoying the privileges that are the outcome of p... injustice, I can become complicit in those heinous acts. If I choos... be willfully ignorant of such harms and make no effort to rem... them and seek out restitution or restoration, then I have com... deserve blame and guilt. True, I am not at all guilty for mys... committing the past injustice, but I am guilty if I make no ef... to bring about restitution (atonement). In the Christus Vic... ransom theory, there has been a bounteous offering by God... all times and ages by which all persons can find a life-saving ... on with God through Christ. What is needed to attain it is to ap... priate it by dying to self and being transfigured into the life of C... Allow me two other thought experiments; these concern how ... might appropriate today either goods or ills of the past.

Imagine you have received an inheritance from a... cle who earned a living by providing affordable housing and... cal care for refugees, combatting climate change through s... energy, establishing fair trade relations with African farmers, ... successfully negotiating a nuclear-free Korean peninsula. On... he conditions of the will is that you use your life to serve the... lic good. You have also received an inheritance from an aunt... involves no commitments on your part, but the aunt's wealth ... e from promoting racially segregated housing, establishing ... dio stations that deny climate change, endorsing the claim t... he USA 2020 election was fraudulent, and claiming that takin... vaccine to combat the pandemic causes sterility and autism. ... and she also benefited from what many believe was sex-traffi... (never absolutely proven). I think we can agree that acceptin... uncle's bequest would be a way of honoring his past good wo... and having the opportunity to magnify it (a nice Marian ter... "My soul doth magnify the Lord . . ."), while accepting the au... bequest would be tainting, unless perhaps you used the wealth to overturn and reverse her noxious work.

Fourth objection: The Christus Victor may be less supernatural than the Gregorian ransom theory insofar as it does not require the belief that Satan exists, but it still requires a massive role for miracles. There is the miracle of the resurrection of Jesus Christ plus the idea that human persons survive death, whether this involves heaven or some life that is not heaven, whatever that might be. It also seems to require there are veridical (trustworthy) experiences of God (and maybe experiences of the risen Christ) in which persons may come to be (or to feel that they are) united in the life of Christ. This is simply beyond belief for educated persons today.

Reply: Consider two replies. The first is predictable. I have argued extensively elsewhere for the plausibility of theism and the evidential power of religious experiences. A full reply would take you and me to other books and articles.[22] I only add here that some of the arguments against the miraculous are so aggressive that they render our ordinary, purposive action (like my writing this book and you reading it) as miracles. I defer to other sources for you to investigate such issues.[23] My second reply is less common: I suggest that we should hope that the Christus Victor ransom theory is true. I concede that if you know with certainty that it is false (like you can know with certainty 2+2=5 is necessarily false), hoping it is true would be nonsense. But if you can't rule it out and it is a live hypothesis, wouldn't it make sense to hope that all the damage, harm, and destruction in world history might be challenged by an omnipotent love capable of redeeming wrongdoers, bringing them to a transfigured identity in the restoration of that which has been lost? Some of this hope may be hinted at in the way some persons express their deep remorse for past injustice.

Consider, for example, the expression of remorse and repentance from the assistant secretary of the Bureau of Indian Affairs

22. See Taliaferro, *The Golden Cord*.

23. See Taliaferro and Evans, *Is God Invisible? As Essay on Religion and Aesthetics*.

in the United States regarding past, shameful acts that were injurious to Native Americans:

> Never again will this agency stand silent when hate and violence are committed against Indians. Never again will we allow policy to proceed from the assumption that Indians possess less human genius that the other races. Never again will we be complicit in the theft of Indian property. Never again will we appoint false leaders who serve purposes other than those of the tribe. Never again will we allow unflattering and stereotypical images of Indian people to deface the halls of government or lead the American people to shallow and ignorant beliefs about Indians. Never again will we attack your religions, your languages, your rituals, or any of your tribal ways. Never again will we seize your children, nor teach them to be ashamed of who they are. Never again.

All this is well and good, but the secretary went on: "We desperately wish we could change history."[24]

As acknowledged earlier, most philosophers believe that the truths about what is now past cannot be altered. There is no being so powerful, not even God, that can make it the case that Native Americans were not abused for centuries by European settlers and their descendants. But there are measures one can take now to restore land, to ensure the continuance of Native American culture and livelihoods, to make sure that our educational institutions teach the truth about past injustices, and more. With its stress on transfiguration through restitution, the Christus Victor ransom theory speaks to the importance of restoration in the here and now, which might form small acts in the greater work of redemption that may take place cosmically, in this life and that which transcends this life.

---

24. Kevin Grover cited by Aaron Lazare in *On Apology*, 109–10.

Chapter Four

Good Bedfellows

*The Ransom Theory and Rival Accounts
of the Atonement*

For the rest of the book, by "ransom theory" I am referring to the Christus Victor ransom theory. Narnian theology will return in chapter five.

Since the early medieval era (roughly, the eleventh century), theories of the atonement have been *any version except the ransom theory*. In this chapter we will consider a host of them. I will be painting with a broad brush, with minimal references, in an effort to favorably sketch these accounts. Afterwards, I will suggest that these accounts are not only compatible with the ransom theory, the ransom theory can provide important support for these so-called rivals.

From Anselm of Canterbury to Eleonore Stump: Any Version Except the Ransom Theory

The Satisfaction Model

Anselm was one of the most important medieval Christian philosophers, with a large following today. Before sketching his account of the atonement, let us take note of his major contribution to the philosophy of God.

Anselm is best known for his understanding of God as "that than which nothing greater can be conceived." That is, God's greatness is unsurpassable or maximal; there *could not* be a being more excellent or praiseworthy than God. Anselmians contend that the divine attributes may be seen as flowing from God's maximal greatness. It is because God is unsurpassably great that God is supremely good, omniscient, omnipotent; God exists necessarily rather than contingently (God's being is not a matter of chance or derived from some higher being) and God is eternal or everlasting. That is, God is either outside of time (God eternally created time) or God is temporal (there is a past, present, and future for God) but without a temporal beginning or end. Anselmian theology is sometimes referred to as *perfect being theology*.

As for the atonement, Anselm's account is often classified as a satisfaction theory. In rough outline, all creatures (or all those created in God's image) owe God gratitude and honor because God has created the cosmos and conserves it in existence (the creation would cease to be if it were not sustained by God's creative will). Because we have not offered God such gratitude and honor, we are indebted to God. This debt is impossible for us to pay, given our frailty, proneness to sin, and other limitations. The gravity of our failing to honor God is proportionate to the greatness of the being to whom honor is due. Because God is maximally great our dishonor is maximally grave. For God simply to forgive us this debt would leave unsatisfied that which is owed to God. Because the debt is owed by humans, God became incarnate as a human being, Jesus Christ, who lived a sinless life of gratitude and honor to God, thus satisfying the debt we owe to God. (This included offering his life, which—as divine—is of infinite value, as a gift of obedience to God. This infinite gift was equal to the infinite debt of honor owed, thus paying it in full.)

This account not only avoids paying a ransom to Satan; there is no role at all for Satan. It affirms the Christian thesis that Jesus Christ is fully human and fully God. Moreover, while Jesus is wholly God (*totus Deus*) Jesus is not the whole of God (*totum Dei*). The distinction in the Godhead of Father, Son, and Holy Spirit, allows the Son to become incarnate and offer his life and work to the Father. The atonement for you and me comes through realizing and faithfully trusting the significance of Jesus' satisfaction on our behalf; it is also worked out in an affective relationship between the soul and Jesus, mortifying vices and cultivating virtues. Sometimes Anselm's account is mistakenly interpreted as Jesus providing a sacrifice to placate the anger of God the Father. Such an interpretation is completely undermined when you take seriously the beautiful, tender portrait that Anselm presents of our relationship with God through Christ. Here is a hymn from the writings of St. Anselm in use today:

1 Jesus, like a mother you gather your people to you;
  you are gentle with us as a mother with her children.

2 Often you weep over our sins and our pride,
  tenderly you draw us from hatred and judgement.

3 You comfort us in sorrow and bind up our wounds,
  in sickness you nurse us, and with pure milk you feed us.

4 Jesus, by your dying we are born to new life;
  by your anguish and labour we come forth in joy.

5 Despair turns to hope through your sweet goodness;
  through your gentleness we find comfort in fear.

6 Your warmth gives life to the dead,
  your touch makes sinners righteous.

7 Lord Jesus, in your mercy heal us;
  in your love and tenderness remake us.

8 In your compassion bring grace and forgiveness,
  for the beauty of heaven may your love prepare us.[1]

The extraordinary intimacy of this understanding of redemption is breathtaking.

---

1. "The Song of Anselm" is available online on the Church of England website: https://www.churchofengland.org/prayer-and-worship/worship-texts-and-resources/common-worship/daily-prayer/canticles-daily-56.

There are elements in this hymn that are very [...] along the lines of the Christus Victor ransom theory: throu[gh] [J]esus we receive new life, the love of Jesus "remakes us."

While Anselm's account is frequently taken to in[... to be] penal substitution, it may plausibly be argued that for Anse[lm] [J]esus' offering is an *alternative* to punishment. On this view, w[e eith]er offer God the honor due to him (which we are incapable of [doin]g) or we face punishment. Jesus' offering to God is the gift of [d]ivine life of infinite value offered on our behalf by our human [r]epresentative (thus, only the God-man could make such an o[fferi]ng). *Yet on Anselm's account Jesus' death is not taking our pu[nish]ment in order to placate divine wrath but offering a gift that we [co]uld never offer, avoiding the need for any punishment.* If Jesus is p[uni]shed for our sins on the cross, as some suggest, that would a[dd poin]t to the *inadequacy* of Jesus' offering. For Anselm, it is Jesus' [offeri]ng as a gift that is saving, not Jesus taking God's anger on our [be]half.

Be that as it may, as the purpose of this chapter i[s to] propose that the Christus Victor theory can supplement other a[cc]ounts, I will not pause to dive into the nuances of which readin[g of] Anselm is the best. Even if Anselm's own account is not comp[at]ible with penal substitution, that does not mean that penal su[bstit]ution is not compatible with the Christus Victor model I defe[nd]. In fact, I think that it is.

The Penal Substitution Model

The Anselmian account has been criticized on the sa[me] ground as another satisfaction theory, one involving punish[ment]. Let us consider this viewpoint and then confront the objecti[on]. On this view, sometimes called the *penal substitution theory* [(al]so called the forensic theory), we deserve punishment by [God] for our sins. The atoning work of Jesus is achieved by him ta[kin]g on the punishment on our behalf. His suffering and death is [the]reby vicarious. Isaiah 53:5 is often cited in support of the p[enal] theory: "But he was pierced for our transgressions, he was cru[she]d for our iniquities; the punishment that brought us peace was on him, and by his wounds we are healed."

Both the Anselmian and penal substitution have been critiqued on the grounds that debts of honor and the punishment owed to a guilty person cannot be transferred to another person. Immanuel Kant, the German philosopher, made the following claim about moral debts:

> [A debt of honor or deserved punishment] is no *transmissible liability* which can be made over to another like a financial indebtedness (where it is all one to the creditor whether the debtor himself pays the debt or whether someone else pays it for him); rather is it *the most personal of all debts*, namely a debt of sins, which only the culprit can bear and which no innocent person can assume even though he be magnanimous enough to wish to take it upon himself for the sake of another.[2]

Is Kant right? If so, this is not obvious to me. In response to Kant, imagine cases when dishonor and wrongdoing have effects that are transmissible. If a colleague in my college has acted dishonorably (grading with favoritism, making claims that border on racism, does not show up for scheduled office hours, and so on) this does seem to me to be something I might well feel shame and perhaps guilt about (imagine that I was a member of the committee that hired the culprit). As chair of the department, I might even (rightly) feel bound to apologize to the students and their parents for having an errant colleague who has tarnished our history, longtime commitments, and integrity. Many such cases can be described in which what Kant refers to as "the most personal of all debts" are not private and isolated, but are attributable to others who may be innocent *as individuals* but who as part of a school, family, city, or culture, share dishonor, shame, or guilt. Cases of when persons may shoulder the debts of honor and moral obligations of others are especially evident in the case of service professionals such as soldiers, police officers, and firefighters. In many cases, these services involve people who (ideally) volunteer to act

2. Kant, *Religion within the Limits of Reason Alone*, 66.

on behalf of fellow citizens to serve the good and justice. Presumably, in a just society, we all have some debt to ensure that persons are free from unjust military invasions, crime, and fires (whether accidental or by arson). Because it is imprudent and not feasible for each of us to pay this debt ourselves by acting in these services, others need to be trained and certified to act on our behalf. We transmit our debt of honor and civil duty to specialists. When they act well, they bring us honor and satisfaction. When they act dishonorably or commit crimes, we can (sometimes) rightly feel liable for their failures.

As a general rule, then, Kant's principle claim is open to question. But let's focus on the specific case of Jesus Christ in the penal theory of the atonement. Imagine that we sinners deserve death. An innocent person, Jesus, agrees to take our place and be killed instead of us. Is this substitution ethically permissible such that Jesus has paid our debt for us? I am inclined to think that our response may rest on some cultural factors. In Kant's early modern Germany there was a staunch individualism, but in other cultures, such as in ancient Israel, matters seem to be different. The later was a context when there could be rites of purification in which an animal is chosen to bear the sins of the people (Lev 18:1–34). It is from this practice that we get the term "scapegoat"—with the animal in question being a goat. Agreed, today in the West, the notion of a scapegoat seems suspect, but why rule out the possibility that an innocent person may shoulder another person's debt of honor or moral obligation? Going back to referencing people in special services, imagine that your neighbor is attacked. You have an obligation to rescue her and subdue the attacker, but you lack the competence to do so and call the police. A police officer arrives, rescues her, but is killed in the process. I suggest this is a case of when an innocent person (the police officer) shoulders your responsibility to rescue those who are endangered and pays for this with her life.

One more response: Kant may be underestimating the nature of what he recognizes as transmissible debts, namely cases of when a third party (call that party Chris) may pay a creditor what you owe to the creditor. Imagine that your debt was legal (not the result of manipulation or exploitation) and that it is enormous. Chris loves you and voluntarily takes on the task of paying your debt for you. The amount you owe might cause Chris to give to your creditor all that Chris owns. Imagine that it causes Chris such an enormous burden that he dies in the process. To make the thought experiment especially vivid, imagine that Chris dies paying off your debt, not only due to his becoming destitute, but due to an accident in the course of Chris selling his blood, donating a kidney for pay, and being paid for donating bone and skin. My point is that this transmissible debt looks very much like the way an innocent person might shoulder the debt owed to another.

The Exemplar Model

Consider another model for the atonement, often called the *exemplar model*. On this view, Jesus Christ was God incarnate, whose birth, life, teaching, miracles, suffering, death, and resurrection displays God's superabundant loving nature. Jesus is no mere example of how we are to live (with compassion, integrity, mercy) but a supreme display of God's love, which powerfully invokes us to follow his path of love. One can find the exemplar model in the Epistle to Diogentus, the Shepherd of Hermas, and the letters of Clement of Rome, Ignatius of Antioch, Clement of Alexandria, Hippolytus of Rome, and the Martyrdom of Polycarp. Here is a passage from the work of St. Clement (died c.215):

> For [Christ] came down, for this he assumed human nature, for this he willingly endured the sufferings of humanity, that be being reduced to the measure of our weakness he might raise us to the measure of his power. And just before he poured out his offering, when he gave himself as a ransom, he left us a new testament: "I give you my love." What is the nature and extent of this love? For each of us he laid down his life, the life which was

worth the whole universe, and he requires in return that
we should do the same for each other.[3]

Clement's referring to Christ as a ransom hints at what I will
claim later, namely that these rival theories of atonement are compatible with the ransom theory, but I cite Clement here for his view
that Christ's powerful self-donation should inspire us to donate
ourselves to God and to one another.

The exemplar model is sometimes considered a subjective
model of the atonement, because of its stress on our subjective
response to the life, death, and resurrection of Jesus. It has mistakenly been attributed to the twelfth-century philosopher Peter
Abelard, who actually accepted a satisfaction model. Still, Abelard
so stressed the affective side of our response to Christ that I think
it fitting to cite his poem, "Solus ad victimam," here as a soulful
witness to Christ's costly love. Notice the solidarity or merging
between our sorrow and the sorrow of Jesus.

> Alone to sacrifice thou goest, Lord, giving thyself to
> Death whom thou hast slain.
> For us thy wretched folk is any word? Who know that for
> our sins this is thy pain?
> For they are ours, O Lord, our deeds, our deeds. Why
> must thou suffer torture for our sin?
> Let our hearts suffer in thy Passion, Lord, that very suffer-
> ing may thy mercy win.
> This is the night of tears, the three days' space, sorrow
> abiding of the eventide,
> Until the day break with the risen Christ, and hearts that
> sorrowed shall be satisfied.
> So may our hearts share in thine anguish, Lord, that they
> may sharers of thy glory be;
> Heavy with weeping may the three days pass, to win the
> laughter of thine Easter Day.[4]

3. Available online: https://www.patheos.com/blogs/tonyjones/2012/03
/14/a-better-atonement-moral-exemplar/.

4. Available online: https://www.stmichaelsmountdinham.org.uk/wp-
content/uploads/2020/04/Solus_ad_victimam_Leighton.pdf.

So-called subjective accounts of the atonement have been criticized on the grounds that they make redemption more of a matter of how we respond to Christ, rather than the work of Christ itself. In my view, that objection misses the mark at least for many advocates of the subjective models. Most "subjective accounts" would be better called inter-subjective or interactive accounts as they involve the mutual activity of Jesus and the soul, of the kind displayed in Abelard's work.

Small concession: some who are classified as advocating an exemplar model do not have such inter-subjective, interaction. Thomas Jefferson, for example. As a deist, Jefferson did not accept the Christian view of the incarnation, and so Jesus was an inspiring exemplar, but no more.

Contemporary Models of the Atonement

Let us now engage some contemporary models for the atonement. Consider the work of Philip Quinn, Richard Purtill, Richard Swinburne, and Eleonore Stump.

Philip Quinn's model

Philip Quinn advances the following parable as a model for Christian atonement.

> Imagine that a great magnate makes his two sons stewards of the two finest farms on his estate. The elder son irresponsibly neglects and thus ruins his farm, while the younger son conscientiously makes his farm flourish. As a result of his negligence, the elder son owes it to his father to make reparations by restoring his farm to its former prosperity. It would be severe but just for the father to punish him by disinheriting him if he does not repair the ruined farm. Unfortunately, the elder son is not a good enough farmer to be able to accomplish this task, though he is good enough that he could have prevented the ruin of the farm had he but tried to do so.

Acknowledging his responsibility and guilt, the elder son repents of his negligence, and sincerely apologizes to his father. But as the father contemplates the now des... fields of the ruined farm, he cannot help thinking that repentance and apology are not enough. He is poised to exercise his right to disinherit his guilty son.

Then the younger son intervenes. Moved by love for his brother as well as by devotion to their father and the welfare of his estate, the younger son undertakes to restore the farm that his brother has ruined to its former prosperity. This new endeavor requires tremendous sacrifices from him; he must maintain his own farm while trying to rehabilitate another. His guilty elder brother joins with him in this undertaking. And then a series tragedy occurs. At harvest time the younger son has to work late into the evening to finish mowing the hay in his brother's fields. Just as he is completing this chore, marauding outlaws catch him in the open, slay him, and set the hay ablaze. His heroic attempt to restore the ruined farm ends in failure. But his sacrifices so work upon the grieving father's heart that he is persuaded to be merciful, rather than severe, toward his surviving elder son. He forgives his elder son for the damage he has done to the estate, even though that damage has not been repaired, and he mercifully refrains from exercising his right to disinherit his erring elder son.[5]

This model has merit. It emphasizes stewardship and creation as a gift. Evil turns out to be a misuse of a gift. The bond between sinner and redeemer is one of fraternity and love. I believe that Quinn rightly highlights the importance of restoration in the cause of redemption and there is also a fitting place for repentance, remorse, apology, and the intent to do better. There is no role for Satan, deception, or the paying of a ransom.

Richard Purtill's model

Consider a slightly different account by Richard Purtill:

---

5. Quinn, "Swinburne on Guilt, Atonement, and Christian Redemption."

A certain king had a jewel which he valued so highly that he had enlisted a band of knights, sworn to safeguard the jewel or die in the attempt. An enemy of the king, desiring the jewel, corrupted the knights one after another, some with bribes, some with threats, and some with promises. Then the enemy carried off the jewel. The king's son, who had been away with his squire while this was happening, returned to find the jewel gone. He went alone into the enemy's stronghold and after great suffering, managed to get the jewel back. On his return the king held court. The forsworn knights came before him to express their sorrow and accept their punishment. The king's son was also there, and his father praised him for his heroism, promising him whatever reward he wished. The prince said to the king, "Father, as my reward I ask that you do not punish the forsworn knights. Let my sufferings in getting back your jewel be all that anyone has to suffer in this matter." The king agreed, but the prince's squire objected, saying "This is to put these traitors on an equal footing with those of us who have not betrayed their king." However, the chief of the forsworn knights replied to him saying, "Sir, we are not on an equal footing with you, but below you in one way and above you in another. You are above us in that you have never betrayed your king, while we are forgiven traitors. But we are above you in that our prince has given us a gift which you have not received from him: his suffering has won our pardon. Therefore we have more reason to love our prince, and more motive to serve him and his father faithfully in the future."[6]

What seems correct in this parable? It treats sin as a kind of theft, or thwarting of something just and right. It gets at the notion that (metaphorically) evil can involve a kind of distance from the good. It sees the redeemer's action as heroic. The resurrection may be hinted at by the metaphor of the jewel being restored, if "jewel" stands for life, i.e., the son brings back to life that which has been ruined. Maybe this is akin to Christ's dying and rising.

---

6. Purtill, "Justice, Mercy, Supererogation, and Atonement," 39.

Richard Swinburne's model

Consider Richard Swinburne's account of the atonement in *Responsibility and Atonement*. Swinburne identifies some the elements that need to come into play in atonement between persons: repentance, apology, reparation, and penance. Some of these elements have been addressed in the Christus Victor ransom theory. The notion of penance has merit in a full account of a healthy reconciliation. Back to chapter three, in a case of minor wrongdoing, only replacing what I have damaged or stolen does not seem to be enough. I need to do more than replace your pen, but to get you dozens of new pens, plus chocolates and flowers perhaps. According to Swinburne, we need to appeal to the work of Jesus Christ when it comes to offering repentance and reparation to God. In a sense, Swinburne is in the Anselmian tradition. God is owed maximal fealty and gratitude for creating and sustaining us in being. We have not and perhaps cannot succeed in this, but Jesus Christ has lived a sinless life of fealty, gratitude, and obedience. The principal, defining moment of the atonement occurs when a repentant sinner offers the life and death of Christ as a perfect sacrifice for what he (and every other human person) owes to God. The one redeemed is accepted by God the Father because the Father accepts the offering of the God-man.

Eleonore Stump's model

Finally, consider Eleonore Stump's model of the atonement in two stages: one from a paper, "Atonement According to Aquinas," and the other from Stump's book *Atonement*.

In her paper, Stump uses the following parable to set up the conditions of atonement:

> Consider two friends, Susan and David. They have been best friends for years, but recently David has become an alcoholic, and he is given to driving while drunk. On one such occasion he had a bad accident while driving with Susan's little daughter Maggie in his car, and, because in

his drunken state he had neglected to buckle the child in, Maggie is killed. If Susan and David are not to be alienated despite this dreadful event, there will be two obstacles to their friendship: first, the problem of dealing with the moral wrong David has done (I will call this the problem of past sin) and, second, the problem of dealing with the moral wrong David is likely to do, given that he is still an alcoholic (I will call this the problem of future sin).[7]

Stump goes on to artfully spell out how David might be transfigured personally by union with Christ, putting off the past sin through repentance.

In her magisterial book *Atonement*, Stump extends her position, using Aquinas' understanding of the two aspects of love: the desire for the good of the beloved and the desire to be united with the beloved. Her view of the consummation of the atonement is a kind of loving reciprocity or mutual indwelling; we are to dwell in God and God is to dwell in us. By her lights, forgiveness is not a major obstacle or stage in the work of atonement, as a God of perfect love will forgive us our sins without conditions (there is no need for Christ to pay a debt of honor or ransom and no need for us to repent in order to be forgiven). The key is a kind of pairing of what theologians may call justification and sanctification in which persons are brought to wanting to will the good. This is achieved through what she calls God's operative and cooperative grace. This suffices to prompt persons to repentance, but it is not strong enough to remove the stain of past wrongdoing, the guilt and shame. For that to occur, Jesus Christ, in his passion, mind-reads all the guilt and shame in the past, present, and future, taking it upon himself, experiencing how this alienates us from God the Father. This may be seen in Christ's cry of dereliction on the cross (Mark 15:34, in which Christ cries out that God has forsaken him). We come to be healed of our sins and harms as the Holy Spirit leads us into union with God, being cleansed by the purging loving presence of the Risen Christ.

---

7. Stump, "Atonement according to Aquinas," 270.

As with the other accounts of atonement in this chapter, there is no role for Satan, ransom, or divine deception. Broadly speaking, her account may be more psychological and gives a more central role to the Holy Spirit than the Anselmian or penal accounts. Interestingly for our purposes in this book, Stump appeals to a fairytale in filling out how mind-reading might work; she references the ways in which Frodo can read other minds in Tolkien's *The Lord of the Rings*.

My goal in this section is not to criticize any of these non-ransom models, so I will only add here what I hope is a friendly suggestion. I am not sure that Stump's account requires that Christ mind-reads all sinners at all times for his sacrifice to be redeeming. The worry is that this kind of omniscient mind-reading would seem out of keeping (but not impossible) with Jesus Christ being fully human (taking on the limitations of human life). It also does not seem required for Jesus' passionate embrace, enduring, and overcoming of guilt and shame to be efficacious. Might it not suffice for Christ to suffer, knowing the shame of wrongful betrayal, without having to grasp every single betrayal that has occurred and will yet occur on our planet?

The Ransom Theory to the Rescue!

I now propose that the ransom theory is not only compatible with the above models of atonement, it can also enhance each of them.

The Anselmian account would be strengthened if it included the claim that part of the atonement consists in the transfiguration through restoration of that which has been lost, damaged, or destroyed. The same is true in the penal theory, and the exemplar theory. Philip Quinn's thought experiment has merit and is plausible but tragic. With the ransom theory the story may have a different ending: The younger brother repaired the older brother's land. He was killed by bandits and died professing his love for his brother and even for the bandits. After three days, the younger brother rose from the dead through the power of their father, who rejoiced at this coming together of the great family. Seeing this, the bandits confessed their sin and undertook the five stages of atone-ment in the Christus Victor ransom theory.

I have the utmost respect for Purtill and his proposed thought experiment. A supplement of the ransom theory might only ex-pand the story. Perhaps some of the knights are killed in their quest for recovering the jewel and the son raises them from the dead. In Swinburne's account, the ransom theory would add the importance of transfiguration through restitution. In Stump's first case, the ransom theory would add that full healing and recovery would involve raising Maggie from the dead or establishing a life beyond life in which all parties might find transfiguration through restitution. Transfiguration through restoration would also be im-portant additions to Stump's more developed account.

The strategy of this book has been different from many books in philosophy. If you pick up a book on the theory of justice or the theory of knowledge, the first part of the book is usually a critique of rival theories. By the time you are halfway through most books you are on the edge of your seat; tell me, please what is justice? what is knowledge? Stump's book on the atonement is excellent and highly recommended, but it is in the tradition of first critiqu-ing rivals before presenting her positive account. I am not claiming this is wrong or merely strategic. And yet I do highlight that my strategy has been to recover or instill appreciation for atonement in Narnia, greater appreciation for the Gregorian ransom theory, and then build a positive case for the Christus Victor ransom theory. The point of this chapter has not been to critique rival theories but to propose that they may be strengthened with the contribution of the Christus Victor ransom theory. You may wish to reject ransom theories for the reasons cited by C. Stephen Evans, as noted in the introduction, because of the role of Satan and deception, but I urge you, please do not throw the baby out with the bathwater. A ran-som theory can be defended without Satan and without deception.

Chapter Five

Redeeming Narnia

This book might end here, just as I ended a present on the atonement in Narnia one late spring evening many years ago at the Oxford C. S. Lewis Society. But, as noted in the introduction, on that occasion I was not expecting objections to the *Chronicles of Narnia* themselves. My critic on that occasion acknowledged that even if the vision of atonement in Narnia between Aslan and Edmund is coherent, the *Chronicles* themselves are "children books" that make them an unsuitable "launching pad serious theology."

There is no point in replying that Lewis did not write the *Chronicles* for children. He did write the books for children, but not *only* for children. In his essay "On Three Ways of writing for Children," Lewis contends that children's stories that can only be appreciated by children are not good stories. His intent to write for *readers of all ages* certainly succeeded for me, as I first encountered the *Chronicles* as a young adult. In any case, this chapter takes up some elements in the *Chronicles* not covered earlier, that may give readers pause (magic, cultural prejudice) and brings to light three dimensions of the *Chronicles* that seem to be excellent stimuli (or launching pads) for mature theological reflection. I conclude with some suggestions about the difference between being *childish* and *being youthful*. A full-throated defense of the *Chronicles* might have been placed at the beginning of this book; indeed, at the outset I do defend the *Chronicles* as respectful members of the noble tradition of fairy tales—but I surmise that by now some readers might be more motivated to consider a reply to the charge that, at the end of the day, they are (in the negative sense) mere children's stories. After all, if I have convinced you that a version of the ransom theory is respectful, the least I can do is to reply to the objection that my chief sources (the *Chronicles* themselves) are somehow unworthy.

While this chapter is a defense of the *Chronicles*, my intent is for it to be neither defensive nor definitive. For example, the first topic, magic is too protean and fascinating to be fully addressed in a sub-section of a chapter! I urge readers to be as open minded as my critic that night, who, after the exchange at the Lewis society in Pusey House invited me and some friends out for further discussion at one of Lewis' favorite pubs, The Eagle and Child (nicknamed the Bird and Baby) where the exchange was free-wheeling and not at all a matter of cut-and-thrust dueling.

Magic

I confess up front that I may not be the most impartial philosopher on the topic of magic. When the Harry Potter books came out I wanted to be a professor at Hogwarts (actually the building where I work at St. Olaf College, Holland Hall, looks like Hogwarts) and teach defense against the dark arts; I undertook a fascinating independent study with a student who is a professional magician; and I have published "A Modest Defense of Magic."[1] Given a certain definition, I believe in magic.

Magic is a key factor in many fairytales. Magic abounds in one of Lewis' favorite fairytales, *The Golden Key* by George MacDonald, and magic is pervasive in the *Chronicles*. Actually, one of the key differences between the genre of fairytales and science fiction is that the later involves some sort of technology (real or imaginary). In the case of magic, events are brought about, not by

---

1. The defense of magic appears in my book *Love. Love. Love. And Other Essays*, 128–31, referenced in the acknowledgements.

technology, but by spells, incantations or simply the intentional power of a magician (or wizard or witch or some other extraordinary being). There are, however, abundant biblical verses condemning magic (for example, Acts 8:9–24; Gal 5:20; Rev 9:21; 18:23; 21:8). It was in light of such verses that some Christians objected to the Harry Potter series.

The way Christians have addressed these condemnations in the past (especially in the Renaissance) is by distinguishing between what they call *black magic* and *white magic*. The former was associated with the demonic, the exercise of evil powers, and necromancy (communicating with the dead). White magic was akin to employing medicine and the enhanced good powers of lovers of wisdom (philosophers) to address maladies like depression or melancholy and to counter black magic. In the fifteenth century it was not unusual for philosophers like Marsilio Ficino to practice magic and so engage in astrology and alchemy.

In my view, the definitions of "magic" in contemporary dictionaries are not very impressive. Here is an amalgamation of current online definitions:

> the secret power of appearing to make impossible things happen by saying special words or doing special things; the power of apparently influencing the course of events by using mysterious or supernatural forces. Magic, sometimes spelled magick, is the application of beliefs, rituals or actions employed in the belief that they can manipulate natural or supernatural beings and forces. It is a category into which have been placed various beliefs and practices sometimes considered separate from both religion and science. [Magic is] tricks that seem to be impossible and that are done by a performer to entertain people.

While I will propose a different definition that does not use terms like "mysterious," "supernatural," "tricks," and "entertainment," it is noticeable that none of these definitions entail that magic is by its very nature wrong. I suppose there is some hint that magic is not ideal, however, insofar as it is described as a tool of manipulation. In that sense, magic would be in opposition to most religious practices such as petitionary prayer. In the later, one may well pray that God will heal someone who is ill, but this is a plea that God will show mercy rather than an attempt to manipulate or control God. Setting out to manipulate God would be to treat God as a subordinate or a pliable human ruler who might be bribed or otherwise controlled.

Here is a proposed definition of magic that would cover magic in Narnia:

> *An event is magical if the event is extraordinary (not normal or usual) and it is intentionally brought about by an agent without the use of technology or any physical mechanism or the employment of other agents who bring about the event.*

Examples from *The Chronicles* include making a land forever winter without it ever being Christmas, creating trees by singing, transforming animals into talking animals, transporting creatures from one spatial world to another, instilling strength by breathing on a person, turning scrap metal into a lamppost, turning a creature into stone or returning them to life, being killed and then rising from the dead, knowing another person's thoughts through mind reading, endowing an object like an apple or a tree with enhanced powers to heal or to prevent a witch from entering a realm, making creatures invisible, changing a boy into a dragon, and so on.

This definition may be too broad for many readers because it might include as "magic" cases of when someone intentionally brings about an event (getting people to dance) by luring them to dance by playing enchanting music. I am prepared for such broad usage; I think charisma may be thought of as a bit magical. When some of my colleagues, like Gordon Marino, give spell-binding lectures, I am inclined to think they are magical. There is some reason to think that Lewis himself believed that magic was needed to confront the secularism of his day. "Spells are used for breaking enchantments as well as inducing them. And you and I have need of the strongest spell that can be found to wake us from the evil enchantment of worldliness which has been laid upon us for nearly a hundred years."[2]

Three minor points: On my proposed definition, events that are thought of as miracles in Christian tradition would be magical, but not all descriptions of magic would be of miracles. Presumably miracles (the rising of Christ from the dead, stories of Jesus healing) are *religiously significant events brought about by God or Jesus as God incarnate or brought about by God through prophets* (Moses, Elijah, etc.); lots of magic in Narnia is not brought about by Aslan. So miracles might be considered a subset of magic.

Second, in a world of magic more events are intentional than in non-magic worlds. In a magical world, there would be the same wide array of intentional events no different from non-magical worlds (people would still walk about, go to work, and so on) but there would *also* be events like trees moving or a river flooding due to a summons by Aslan to rouse the tree creatures and a river god to join in the battle with the Telmarines.

Third, in several scenes in the *Chronicles*, creatures are given different bodies. In *Magician*, Strawberry is re-named Fledge and turned into a flying horse. In *Voyage*, Eustace is turned into a dragon. In *Horse*, when Prince Rabadash's plot to invade Archenland and Narnia is exposed and overturned, Aslan turns him into an ass. Because only philosophers, indeed maybe only those practicing philosophy of mind, would have an interest in this curious topic, my comment will be brief. Significant philosophers contend that the key to personal identity over time is the continued persistence of our material bodies. Because of this, some of these philosophers deny persons can persist in being after bodily death. There are many reasons to resist such a form of materialism, but I note here that our ease of imagining persons undergoing radical metamorphosis is reason to believe that we can conceive of personal identity persisting despite radical physical change.

In this first section, I hope enough has been said for you to be open (in principle) to magic and not charge that magic is always and only the devil's business.

2. *The C. S. Lewis Readers Encyclopedia*, 121.

Prejudices

Are there cultural or racial prejudices in the *Chronicles*? A simple search of the web offer multiple ostensible cases and replies from fans of Narnia. I have already replied to the objection that Lewis mistreats Susan in *Battle*. On other matters: it is true that all the human characters who travel to Narnia from our world are white, but Narnia is the most diverse world possible in terms of species and races. In *Caspian*, Lewis even has a heroic character Doctor Cornelius who is of a mixed-race, half dwarf, who is honored by the future King of Narnia, notwithstanding there being a prejudice by dwarfs of inter-marriage. In terms of gender, the Witch is, of course, female, but the arch-evil force in *Battle* is male and in each book there is at least one female character who is bold, good, courageous, sometimes completely outshining her male counterpart (especially in *Magician*). The Kingdom of Narnia is monarchical; in *Lion*, the four children are made kings and queens, and this has hereditary consequences (while the four children do not have children, in *Caspian* it is assumed that royalty is by descent). I can certainly understand how an advocate of republicanism (the denial of monarchy) might take umbrage to Narnian governance, but I suggest that monarchy in Narnia is similar to monarchy in Tolkien's *The Lord of the Rings*, an ideal, non-authoritarian leadership that requires justice, humility, and sacrificial service to the people. I believe that Lewis and Tolkien created imaginary worlds that were not made as a blueprint for political structures in our world. (As an aside, when it comes to our world, as opposed to Middle Earth, Tolkien leaned towards anarchism.)

So, I suggest that many of the charges of prejudice in the *Chronicles* are off-beam. More serious, though, is the treatment of the Calormenes as black or dark-skinned versus the fair-skinned or white Narnians. In fact, in *Battle* there is a scene that may conjure up the practice of black face (the widely condemned practice of white persons masquerading as black persons). The King of Narnia and children make their skin dark to disguise themselves as Calormenes. The disguise is so effective that when a dwarf sees

them, he refers to them as "darkies" (chapter 11). This   y needs
to be offset by four factors.

First, not all Narnians are white. There is a myri   talking
beasts (beavers, bears, owls, and so on) that are not w

Second, the King and children are making thei   s black
as a disguise in an effort to free Narnia from an unju   vading,
Calormene army. They are not at all engaged in raci   icature
(as in the practice of "black face" today). It is a dwa   o calls
the King and children "darkies," and it is natural for u   nterpret
this as a derisive term that does not deserve our respe   ead the
incident as Lewis intentionally condemning such raci   ision.

Third, *Horse* ends with the marriage of Arvis, a   ormine,
and Shasta, a Narnian. They are recognized as a go   ng and
queen and their mixed-race son becomes the most fa   king of
Archenland.

Finally, in *Battle*, we see that salvation or fulfill   t is not
exclusively for Narnians (of whatever color, white chil   brown
bears, golden lions, black owls., . . .) or those who kno   ly serve
Aslan. A Calormene named Emeth who served the   Tash is
welcomed by Aslan. In an exchange between Emeth an   lan, we
learn that whether you live in harmony with Aslan is   matter
only of whether you serve a being you name "Aslan." I   be that
you think you are serving Aslan but because your li   o alien
from Aslan's way of love, you are not. Alternatively, yo   y think
you are serving an alien god, but in real life you are on   n's side.

Because some object to Christianity and its supp   l exclu-
sionary vision of salvation, I offer two comments here

Over centuries, Christians have differed on whetl   alvation
can be secured only through one's explicit professio   faith in
Christ in this life. Some Christians resist such a restri   n: what
about the death of children or the lives of persons wh   ve never
heard of Christ? If Aslan in Narnia should be our guid   e saving
love of God and for God may extend far beyond expli   l, Christian boundaries.

This Narnian theology also speaks to some co   nporary
reflection on the difference between atheists and th   s. It has

been observed that there is a distinction between *theoretical* and *practical* atheism and theism. A person might claim to be an atheist and this is quite accurate at a theoretical level, but they live a life that is very much in keeping with, say, Christian theism: they treat the world as sacred, they seek to live a life of mercy and justice, they care deeply for the vulnerable. On the other hand, there may be a professing Christian theist, but whose practical life is more in keeping with the denial of God, the source of goodness; they ignore the vulnerable and traffic in lies and exploitation.

I now turn from responding to objections to highlighting three positive elements in the *Chronicles* for mature, serious theology.

Three Launching Pads

A. A Trilemma in Context

I suggest that the trilemma that is set forth in the *Chronicles* is filled out in a way that is especially illuminating as it takes into account the broader, important context in which we assess whether some testimony is reliable.

In one of Lewis' mature books for adults, *Mere Christianity*, he is famous for challenging those who claim that Jesus was a great moral teacher, but not God incarnate. He presents a trilemma (a three-way choice): given the claims that Jesus makes (principally, his claim to divinity), we should not think of Jesus as a great moral teacher; rather, we should think that Jesus' claim is true or, if it is false, conclude that Jesus is either a liar or insane.

> I am trying to prevent anyone from saying the really foolish thing that people often say about Him: "I'm ready to accept Jesus as a great moral teacher, but I don't accept His claim to be God." That is the one thing we must not say. A man who was merely a man and said the sort of things Jesus said would not be a great moral teacher. He would either be a lunatic—on a level with the man who says he is a poached egg—or else he would be the Devil of Hell. You must make your choice. Either this

man was, and is, the Son of God: or else a madman or
something worse. You can shut Him up for a fool, you
can spit at Him and kill Him as a demon; or you can fall
at His feet and call Him Lord and God. But let us not
come with patronising nonsense about His being a great
human teacher. He has not left that open to us. He did
not intend to. . . .

   We are faced, then, with a frightening alternative.
This man we are talking about either was (and is) just
what He said or else a lunatic, or something worse. Now
it seems to me obvious that He was neither a lunatic nor
a fiend: and consequently, however strange or terrifying
or unlikely it may seem, I have to accept the view that He
was and is God. God has landed on this enemy-occupied
world in human form.[3]

Some philosophers accept Lewis' trilemma, but others cast
doubts on whether there are only three choices. Perhaps Jesus
honestly believed on the basis of some evidence (visions, fulfilled
prophecies) that he was divine, but he was nonetheless mistaken.
In that case, Jesus might be neither evil nor insane, but simply
wrong. Or perhaps Jesus' claim to be divine was not *his* claim, but a
claim that was attributed to him by his disciples. What these objections bring to light is that when assessing truth of some claims it is
vital to take into account the context, including one's background
beliefs about reality and trustworthiness. This is a factor that is
addressed in the *Chronicles*.

   In *Lion*, Peter and Susan hear from Lucy that Narnia is real
and that Edmund has been to Narnia, but they hear from Edmund
that he has not been to Narnia. They consult the Professor, who
proposes that they face three alternatives or a trilemma. They may
think or assume Lucy is lying or that she is mad or that she is telling the truth. In what follows I suggest that in the context of the
Chronicles, the Professor's challenge makes sense and supports a
general maxim that *when assessing testimony one needs to take seriously background beliefs about what is possible or probable.*

---

3. Lewis, *Mere Christianity*, 55–56; see also Davis, "Was Jesus Mad, Bad, or
God?" and Horner, "*Aut Deus aut Malus Homo.*"

In their response to the Professor, Peter and Susan reply claiming that Lucy must not be telling the truth because, when they look into the wardrobe, they do not see another world. They also observe that Lucy's story is also unlikely because she claims to have been in Narnia some stretch of time, when very little time had elapsed. The Professor responds that these facts actually *support* Lucy's story. He tells them that if there were another realm or world that Lucy entered, it would not be surprising if entry into that world would be peculiar (not a matter of going to that world through an ordinary hallway), nor would it be strange if in that world time was different from our world. If Lucy was fabricating a story about Narnia, wouldn't she have simply not included the idea of Narnia being in a different time zone and simply remain hidden from her siblings for longer. The Professor asks Peter and Susan whether they think her story about Narnia is the sort of thing that a person her age would simply make up. They also admit that Lucy is not the kind of person who would lie. She has a history of only telling the truth. Edmund is less credible.

What is missing from the trilemma of the *Chronicles* is the option that Lucy did not really make the claims she did. Moreover, in the context of the books, we have reasons to trust that Lucy, unlike Edmund, has been reliable in the past. So, under the circumstances laid out in *Lion*, should Lucy be trusted? The Professor would certainly have reason to trust Lucy.

In *Magician*, the book about the creation of Narnia, we learn that before becoming the Professor, he was the boy, Digory Kirke, who was born in 1888 and traveled to Narnia with Polly Plummer by magical rings in 1900. He also knew that the wardrobe was made from the wood that grew from a magical Narnian apple, and so he had some independent reason to think the wardrobe might have magical properties. Given that background experience, Lucy's story is eminently reasonable. But would it be reasonable to believe Lucy's story without such background evidence? I think that depends on your views about space and your evidence of Lucy's trustworthiness.

Lucy describes her entering a realm of space that is not some spatial distance from our world. Narnia is not, say, a mile or a trillion miles from where you are reading this book. We ordinarily assume the unity of space—all spatial objects are some distance from the spatial objects around us. But this is open to challenge, as the philosopher Richard Purtill has argued. In *Reason to Believe: Why Faith Makes Sense*, Purtill points out that in our dream experiences we encounter a visual world (often in color) that is distinct from the spatial world we are in; my image of a tiger in my dream last night was neither in my brain (no observation of my brain will discover a tiger roaming about—or at least I hope not) nor floating above my bed. And yet it was real. True, if you dreamed about running from a tiger, you were not really running from a real tiger, but if dreams are real (that is, people really have dream experiences) then there are spatial objects (objects in your visual field, however fleeting) not spatially some distance from your body and the spatial things of this world. Given that you are open to there being realms distinct from our material world, you might be more receptive to Lucy's story. What also might be on her side is if her story is internally consistent with lots of details and there was no sign that she spent time making up the whole narrative. It took Lewis, age fifty-two at the time, a year to write *Lion* with all its details. In the story itself, would it be credible to believe that Lucy as an eight year old would come up with a detailed claim on the spot (for while she was in Narnia for hours, she was not absent for more than a second or so in our time) that she went through a wardrobe and found herself in a snowy clearing where she met a faun by a lamppost with an umbrella, carrying packages? The improbability of her simply lying or making up the story as a prank plus her past trustworthiness and evident sanity may be enough to make one at least open to the possibility that Narnia is a live hypothesis.

I suggest, then, the *Chronicles* addresses the trilemma argument with an important contribution for mature reflection on how background beliefs can impact our assessment of testimony. The original trilemma of responding to Jesus' claims to be divine would be enhanced for those who, as part of their background beliefs included the conviction that theism is true and that God has some reason to become incarnated, to share in human suffering, and to bring about an atonement between God and creation. This forms a major part of Richard Swinburne's case for Jesus being God incarnate.[4]

I close this section with a suggestion about the bizarre nature of Lucy's claim to visit Narnia: sometimes the bizarre nature of a report can be a reason to believe it, but sometimes not. If a student skipped a class, I would not accept some bizarre accounts (e.g., they were abducted by aliens and returned to campus after class was over) without a huge amount of evidence, but some accounts I have accepted on the grounds of their peculiarity. Ages ago a student told me she missed my class because she delivered a baby in a nearby arboretum. I knew she was a runner and it was likely she ran in the arboretum frequently. There are many walkers in the arboretum, and it would not surprise me that some are pregnant, even near a due date. I accepted her story without any request for evidence because it would have been easier for her to have come up with a less bizarre story (she helped out someone who was lost, she was on the phone with a friend struggling with depression, etc.). I have forgotten her name; if you are that former student, please contact me to let me know whether your story was true!

B. A Wager Argument in Perspective

In the seventeenth century the philosopher-mathematician Blaise Pascal proposed that if one is uncertain whether God exists, one should wager that God exists. Very roughly, the idea is that if there is a God and you wager that God does not exist, the consequences will be horrific. If there is no God and you have wagered that God exists, the consequences are not grave; perhaps you lived a life of sacrificial love in accord with Jesus' teachings. If God does not exist and you wager God does not exist, the outcome is negligible. So, if you wish to maximize the best outcome under conditions of

4. Swinburne, *Was Jesus God?*

uncertainty, you should wager that God exists for that might well be the path to infinite satisfaction if indeed God exists.

Pascal's version of the argument is far more nuanced than I can display here, but it will have to suffice here along with noting the many objections that have been raised against it: there is the so-called "many Gods objection" (how do you know which God to wager on?); the wager presupposes that you can indeed wager, which requires that you control your beliefs, and perhaps that is not possible; the wager seems self-centered and thus not particularly honorable ethically or religiously (why is all the focus on maximizing your well-being?). Perhaps, if there is a God, God would not condemn those who honestly think there is insufficient evidence for God's reality.[5] Debate over Pascal's wager and its progeny (William James crafted a compelling version) continues, but in this context I propose that in *Chair* there is a similar argument that addresses each of the main objections. In fact, notwithstanding that *Chair*, like the other Narnian books, is written for children, it hints at arguments stemming from Feuerbach and Freud that are very much the preoccupation of contemporary, adult philosophers.

In *Chair*, Eustace, Jill, and their charming companion Puddleglum the Marsh-wiggle are led by the Lady of the Green Kirtle (who is actually a witch) to a room in Underland. The Lady or Queen tells them and her captive, Prince Rilian, that the outer world with its sun is a mere projection on their part. Indeed, she claims, so is Aslan, who is only a projection based on their experience of cats. The Lady or Witch develops a projection theory, straight out of work by Freud and Feuerbach. Stories about Aslan or God are childish projections that are designed to provide us with comfort, whereas those who are mature can properly face the fact of our Godless world.

In response, Puddleglum does something bold. He puts his foot in the fire. This seems to interrupt the Witch's spell not only because his act was so shocking, but the odor from his burned foot was bracing! Perhaps he was juxtaposing the evident reality of

---

5. For a recent defense of Pascal's wager, see Rota, *Taking Pascal's Wager*.

pain and smell with the more dreamy spell of the Witch designed to lure them into doubting what they thought were memories of Aslan and Narnia. Puddleglum makes this reply to the Witch: even if Aslan and Narnia are mere projections, he is going to live as though they exist. He will live and die a Narnian, even if there is no Narnia. He finds the apparent goodness of Aslan worth living for, rather than settle for a gloomy underworld. After this, the Witch's true identity is revealed and when she seeks to kill Jill and the others, she is destroyed.

In Puddleglum's wager, note that there is no self-interest or selfishness. Puddleglum is attesting to the ostensible beauty and vibrant goodness of Aslan and the Overland. By standing up for Narnia, he may be seen as seeking solidarity with other Narnians (if there are any) rather than seeking to maximize his well-being. The many Gods objection is circumvented in the context of *Chair*. Sometimes cases can arise in the context of a wager when there are simply two choices; for example, one may need to wager on whether or not to trust someone who is an apparent friend, but one is uncertain. In Puddleglum's case we also have a plausible account of the psychology of wagering; one's beliefs may or may not be directly under one's control, but he (and we) seem to have a choice on whom or what to trust. In *Chair* I suggest we have a plausible case of when someone is professing his loyalty—in this case loyalty to Aslan and the Overland (wagering or betting that they are real)—even in the face of doubt and a paucity of evidence.

We can take some of the details from *Chair* to revise a theistic wager by addressing a person who has evidence that, say, the two most plausible hypotheses they are considering are Christian theism and secular naturalism. We can explicitly rule out an appeal to self-interest by crafting a wager that Christianity is true is to wager that we are made to love others and the creation itself.

I add just three further points.

First, wagering on relationships, values, and worldviews is not at all uncommon. Many of your relationships may be healthy and mutually satisfying, but do you know this with 100% certainty? In many relationships we may be described as betting they are true and good. Similarly, one may have deep loyalty for some values and a view of reality that is not a matter of simply following what you intellectually think is probably true. There are realms of life when probability may be quantitatively precise and confirmed, but in matters of the heart we may have to rely on intuition, emotional sensitivity, and our sense of beauty and ugliness in forging our commitments and loyalties. It may also be noted that there are domains in which we have overriding principles that can guide us when facing situations in which the evidence may be equally balanced for and against a proposition. So, in a court of law, the evidence that a person is guilty of a crime may be significant, but unless it is beyond a reasonable doubt, they should not be convicted. Back to Narnia, Puddleglum may be interpreted as claiming that, short of decisive evidence that Narnia does not exist, it is still good for us to search for it in good faith.

A second point is a bit speculative. It may be that when Puddleglum professes to live like a Narnian even if Narnia does not exist, he may be hinting that, deep down, he is aware of the reality of Narnia even if he can't prove he is right. Perhaps not, but consider the following Puddleglum-like situation: when I correspond with Veronika, a German philosopher, we sign off as "Your friend, even if there is no such thing as friendship." We do this, because some radical philosophers contend that our ordinary assumptions (consciousness, beliefs, and desires exist) are false. Veronika and I have pledged to be friends, come what may. And it may be that our sense of the reality of friendship counts as some evidence (or awareness) that those radical philosophers are wrong

Third, I suggest that the Witch's speech and Puddleglum's reply should be read in every class that addresses wager arguments in philosophy of religion.

C. A Narnian Environmental Ethic

One of the grave threats facing us today is climate change. This threat covers a host of concerns for people of all ages: the effects of pollution, habitation, depopulated areas as a result of rising ocean levels, famine, and more. I suggest that the *Chronicles* offer a vision of the natural world that can bolster our commitment to the wellbeing of our planet. The *Chronicles* present us with a natural world that is created good. In *Magician*, Narnia comes into being through Aslan's singing.

A Narnian environmental ethic is one that stresses good stewardship of the natural world, resistance to tyranny and injustice, respecting the dignity of individual persons, past, present, and future. Some of us can wind up discounting future generations and giving primacy to our own use of land and other resources, whereas Aslan (in *Magician* especially) calls us to care about future generations for their own sake. It is also noteworthy that Aslan calls creatures to a life of joy, as well as of justice and mercy. This suggests that we are called to be motivated by a love of the good, rather than a fear and hatred of that which is evil. In short, Narnia provides a great launching pad for a positive, life-affirming vision of our place in the natural world that we would do well to integrate into our own environmental ethics today.

A brief word on a Narnian environmental ethic concerning nonhuman animals is in order. Although it would be hard to build an animal liberation movement that made vegetarianism compulsory based on the *Chronicles*, the following seem to be contrary to the Narnian way of life: animal cruelty, industrial animal agriculture, and the killing and using of animals that display intelligence, communication, and love.

Being Childish and Being Young

In this final chapter I have not denied that the *Chronicles* are children's books, but I have labored to contend that they contain wisdom, both in terms of a Narnian vision of atonement as well as many other issues for mature reflection on Christian theology and beyond. If by "childish" we mean something like being selfish, immature, impulsive, given over to thoughtless acts, and sulky, then there is nothing childish about the *Chronicles*. Yes, some of its characters are sometimes childish (think of Eustace in *Voyage*), but they are often reformed or purged through transformation (except for some, like the group of skeptical dwarfs in *Battle*). In closing this chapter, I will draw on Plato as I juxtapose being childish and being youthful.

In his epic masterpiece the *Republic*, Plato portrays Socrates in the company of young people meeting in the house of an aging patrician. The old man speaks of his condition as settled; he is not caught up in the passion of desire. Socrates finds him ill-suited for the exciting practice of philosophy. He turns instead to the young people who are filled with desire; they are searching for answers to questions about justice and truth, goodness and evil, education and government, the relationship of men and women, family and children, and more. I suggest that one of the distinctive traits of being young involves raising such questions and searching for answers. In this sense, I propose that the *Chronicles of Narnia* are "youthful" as opposed to "childish" or what we might call juvenile.

The Platonic portrait of youthfulness is not age-specific. You may have the rush of Platonic desire for truth and goodness at any age. Maybe this is one reason why many of us respect some older people, such as C. S. Lewis who wrote the *Chronicles* in his fifties. The reason might not be a matter of him having aged or being old. It may rather be that we can see that Lewis, and some others of his age and beyond, have been youthful for more time than most of us. Thank heavens he has gifted us with the *Chronicles*, work that can awaken the youthfulness of readers of any age.

Bibliography

Aelred of Rievaulx. *Spiritual Friendship.* Translated by M. E. Laker. Kalamazoo, MI: Cistercian, 1977.

Alighieri, Dante. *Dante's Inferno.* Bloomington: Indiana University Press, 1971.

————. *Dante's Purgatorio.* London: Macmillan, 1938.

————. *The Paradiso of Dante Alighieri.* London: Dent, 1921.

Aquinas, Thomas. *Commentary on the Letters of Saint Paul to the Corinthians.* Translated by F. R. Larcher OP, B. Mortensen, and D. Keating, and edited by J. Mortensen and E. Alarcon. Lander, WY: The Aquinas Institute for the Study of Sacred Doctrine, 2012.

Ballard, Jamie. "About Half of Americans Believe Ghosts and Demons Exist." YouGovAmerica. https://today.yougov.com/topics/philosophy/articles-reports/2020/10/30/ghosts-demons-exist-poll-data (accessed March 31, 2022).

Barnes, Richard. "Solus ad Victimam." https://www.stmichaelsmountdinham.org.uk/wp-content/uploads/2020/04/Solus_ad_victimam_Leighton.pdf (accessed March 31, 2022).

Berger, Peter. *A Rumor of Angels: Modern Society and the Rediscovery of the Supernatural.* Garden City, NY: Anchor, 1970.

Chang, Iris. *The Rape of Nanking: The Forgotten Holocaust of World War II.* New York: Basic, 1998.

Chesterton, G. K. "Introduction to the Book of Job." The Society of G. K. Chesterton. https://www.chesterton.org/introduction-to-job/ (accessed April 1, 2022).

————. "On Fairy Tales." Excellence in Literature. https://excellence-in-literature.com/fairy-tales-essay-by-g-k-chesterton/ (accessed April 1, 2022).

————. "The Romance of Childhood." In *In Defense of Sanity,* edited by Dale Ahlquist et al., 250–53. San Francisco: Ignatius, 2011.

Chisholm, Roderick. *Ethics and Intrinsic Value.* Heidelberg: Universitatsverlag, 2001.

Clark, Stephen R. L. *Plotinus: Myth, Metaphor, and Philosophical Practice.* Chicago: University of Chicago Press, 2016.

———. "Why We Believe in Fairies." *First Things*. https://www.fi   1 ings.com/article/2017/03/why-we-believe-in-fairies (accessed April   2).

Clement. *Letter to Corinthians*. In *The Roots of Christian Mystic   xts from the Patristic Era with Commentary*, edited by Olivier Clement   8. New York: New York City Press, 1992.

Clement, Oliver, ed. *The Roots of Christian Mysticism: Texts fra   Patristic Era with Commentary*. New York: New York City Press, 199

Climacus, John. *The Ladder of Divine Ascent*. Translated by C.   id. New York: Paulist, 1982.

Davis, Stephen. "Was Jesus Mad, Bad, or God?" In *The Incarna   , edited by S. Davis, D. Kendall, G. O'Collins, 221–45. New York: Oxf   niversity Press, 2002.

Davison, Andrew. *Participation in God: A Study in Christian   irine and Metaphysics*. Cambridge: Cambridge University Press, 2019

Dickerson, Matthew, and David O'Hara. *Narnia and the Fi   of Arbol*. Lexington, KY: University of Kentucky Press, 2009.

Didache or *Teaching of the Twelve Apostles*. In *The Faith of the   Fathers*, selected and translated by W. A. Jurgens, 1–6. Collegeville,   iturgical, 1970.

Evans, C. Stephen. *A History of Western Philosophy: From the   ocratics to Postmodernism*. Downers Grove, IL: InterVarsity Press, 201

Freeman, Stephan. "St. Gregory the Theologian on Our Ran   by God." https://blogs.ancientfaith.com/glory2godforallthings/2   1/22/st-gregory-the-theologian-on-our-ransom-by-god/ (accesse   March 2022).

Goetz, Stewart. *C. S. Lewis*. Oxford: Blackwell, 2018.

———. "Is N.T. Wright Right about Substance Dualism?" *Phil   a Christi* 4.1 (2012) 183–92.

———. *A Walking Tour with C. S. Lewis: Why It Did Not   le Rome*. London: Bloomsbury, 2014.

Goetz, Stewart, and Charles Taliaferro. *Naturalism*. Grand Rapi   rdmans, 2008.

Graham, Gordon. "Atonement." In *The Cambridge Companio   Christian Philosophical Theology*, edited by Charles Taliaferro and   Meister, 124–35. Cambridge: Cambridge University Press, 2010.

Gregory of Nazianzen. *Collection*. No loc: Aeterna, 2016.

———. *Third Theological Oration*. In *The Roots of Christian My   n*, edited by Olivier Clement, 42–44. New York: Paulist, 1978.

Gregory of Nyssa. *The Life of Moses*. Translated by A. Malherbe an   erguson. In *The Roots of Christian Mysticism*, edited by Olivier Cl   , 24–25. New York: Paulist Press, 1978.

Guthrie, Shandon. *Gods of This World: A Philosophical Discussio   Defense of Christian Demonology*. Eugene, OR: Pickwick, 2018.

Hampton, Alexander, and John Kenney, eds. *Christian Platoni   History*. Cambridge: Cambridge University Press, 2021.

Harper, Ralph. *Sleeping Beauty and Other Essays.* Cambridge, MA: Cowley, 1985.

Hooper, Walter. *C. S. Lewis: A Companion & Guide.* San Francisco: Harper Collins, 1996.

Horner, David. "*Aut Deus aut Malus Homo*; A Defense of C.S. Lewis's 'Shocking Alternative.'" In *C.S. Lewis as Philosopher: Truth, Goodness and Beauty*, edited by D. Baggett, G.R. Habermas, J. Walls, 68–84. Downers Grove, IL: IVP, 2012.

Irenaeus. *Against Heretics.* In *The Roots of Christian Mysticism: Texts from the Patristic Era with Commentary*, edited by Olivier Clement, 86–87. New York: New York City Press, 1992.

Isaac of Nineveh. *Ascetic Treatises.* In *The Roots of Christian Mysticism: Texts from the Patristic Era with Commentary*, edited by Olivier Clement, 297–303. New York: New York City Press, 1992.

Jones, Tony. "A Better Atonement: Moral Exemplar." Theoblogy. https://www.patheos.com/blogs/tonyjones/2012/03/14/a-better-atonement-moral-exemplar/ (accessed March 31, 2022).

Kant, Immanuel. *Religion within the Limits of Reason Alone.* Translated by T. M. Greene and H. H. Hudson. New York: Harper Torchbooks, 1960.

Kreeft, Peter. *Between Heaven and Hell: A Dialogue Somewhere beyond Death with John F. Kennedy, C. S. Lewis, and Alduous Huxley.* Downers Grove, IL: InterVarsity, 2021.

Lazare, Aaron. *On Apology.* Oxford: Oxford University Press, 2004.

Lewis, C. S. *The Complete Chronicles of Narnia.* United Kingdom: HarperCollins, 2006.

———. *The Great Divorce.* London: Macmillan, 2008.

———. *Mere Christianity.* Rev. ed. New York: MacMillan, 1952.

———. *A Preface to Paradise Lost* in *C. S. Lewis: A Companion & Guide.* San Francisco: Harper Collins, 1996.

MacSwain, Robert, and Michael Ward, eds. *The Cambridge Companion to C. S. Lewis.* Cambridge: Cambridge University Press, 2010.

Marlowe, Christopher. *Dr. Faustus.* Mineola, NY: Dover, 2012.

Maximus the Confessor. *Centuries on Charity.* In *The Roots of Christian Mysticism*, edited by Olivier Clement, 276–77. New York: Paulist, 1978.

———. *Questions to Thalassius.* In *The Roots of Christian Mysticism*, edited by Olivier Clement, 38–40. New York: Paulist, 1978.

May, Ashley. "How Many People Believe in Ghosts or Dead Spirits?" *USA Today.* https://www.usatoday.com/story/news/nation-now/2017/10/25/how-many-people-believe-ghosts-dead-spirits/794215001/ (accessed March 31, 2022).

Mellema, Gregory. *Sin.* South Bend, IN: University of Notre Dame Press, 2021.

Miller, J. Steve. *Near-Death Experiences as Evidence for the Existence of God and Heaven.* Acworth, GA: Wisdom Creek, 2012.

Parry, Robin A., with Ilaria Ramelli. *A Larger Hope? Vol. 2, Universal Salvation from the Reformation to the Nineteenth Century*. Eugene, OR: Cascade, 2019.

Peterson, Michael. *C. S. Lewis and the Christian Worldview*. Oxford: Oxford University Press, 2020.

Purtil, Richard. "C. S. Lewis." In *Encyclopedia of Philosophy*, Vol. 5, 2nd ed., edited by D. M. Borchert, 311–13. New York: Macmillan, 2006.

———. *C.S. Lewis and the Case for Christianity*. San Francisco: HarperCollins, 1981.

———. "Justice, Mercy, Supererogation, and Atonement." In *Christian Philosophy*, edited by Thomas P. Flint, 37–50. Notre Dame, IN: University of Notre Dame Press, 1990.

———. *Reason to Believe: Why Faith Makes Sense*. New York: Ignatius, 2009.

Quinn, Philip L. "Swinburne on Guilt, Atonement, and Christian Redemption." In *Reason and the Christian Religion*, edited by A. Padgett, 277–300. Oxford: Oxford University Press, 1994.

Ramelli, Ilaria L. E. *A Larger Hope? Vol. 1. Universal Salvation from Christian Beginnings to Julian of Norwich*. Eugene, OR: Cascade, 2019.

Rea, Michael, ed. *Oxford Readings in Philosophical Theology*, Vol. 1. Oxford: Oxford University Press, 2009.

Reasoner, Paul. "The Double-Movement in Buddhist and Christian Rituals." *European Journal for Philosophy of Religion* 1 (2009) 27–39.

Rota, Michael. *Taking Pascal's Wager: Faith, Evidence, and the Abundance of Life*. Downers Grove, IL: IVP, 2016.

Ruse, Michael. *Can a Darwinian Be a Christian?* Cambridge: Cambridge University Press, 2001.

Russell, Bertrand. "On Being Modern-Minded." In *The Oxford Book of Essays*, edited by John Gross, 351–55. Oxford: Oxford University Press, 1992.

Sartre, Jean-Paul. *No Exit*. Translated by Paul Bowles. New York: Samuel French, 1958.

Schultz, Jeffrey, and John West. *The C. S. Lewis Readers' Encyclopedia*. Grand Rapids: Zondervan, 1998.

Shakespeare, William. *Cymbeline*. London: Royal Victorian Institute for the Blind Tertiary Resource Service, 1955.

———. *Hamlet, Prince of Denmark*. Edited by David Bevington and David Scott Kastan. New York: Bantam Dell, 1988.

———. *The Winter's Tale*. New York: The Royal Shakespeare Company, 2009.

Sheler, L. "Hell's Sober Comeback." *U.S. Daily News and World Report*, March 25, 1991.

"A Song of Anselm." Prayer on Church of England website. https://www.churchofengland.org/prayer-and-worship/worship-texts-and-resources/common-worship/daily-prayer/canticles-daily-56 (accessed March 31, 2022).

Stromberg, Matt. "Gregory of Nyssa: Ransom." Property of Jesus. http://thepropertyofjesus.blogspot.com/2011/03/gregory-of-nyssa-ransom.html (accessed March 31, 2022).

Stump, Eleonore. *Atonement*. Oxford: Oxford University Press, 2018.

————. "Atonement according to Aquinas." In *Philosophy and the Christian Faith*, edited by Michael Rae, 267–93. South Bend, IN: University of Notre Dame Press, 1988.

Swinburne, Richard. *Responsibility and Atonement*. Oxford: Clarendon, 1989.

————. *Was Jesus God?* Oxford: Oxford University Pres, 2010.

Taliaferro, Charles. "Afterlife" In *The Stanford Encyclopedia of Philosophy*, 2019. https://plato.stanford.edu/entries/afterlife/#:~:text=One%20of%20the%20points%20where,nature%20and%20significance%20of%20death.

————. *Cascade Companion to Evil*. Eugene, OR: Cascade, 2020.

————. *The Golden Cord: A Short Book on the Secular and the Sacred*. South Bend, IN: University of Notre Dame Press, 2012.

————. *Love. Love. Love: Light Reflections on Love, Life, and Death*. Cambridge, MA: Cowley, 2006.

————. "A Narnian Theory of the Atonement" *Scottish Journal of Theology* 41.1 (1988) 75–92.

————. *Praying with C. S. Lewis: Companions for the Journey*. Winona, MN: Saint Mary's Press, 1998.

————. "The Real Secret of the Phoenix: Moral Regeneration though Death." In *The Ultimate Harry Potter and Philosophy: Hogwarts for Muggles*, edited by Gregory Bassham, 229–45. Hoboken, NJ: Wiley, 2010.

————. "Religious Rites." In *The Cambridge Companion to Christian Philosophical Theology*, edited by Charles Taliaferro and Chad Meister, 193–200. Cambridge: Cambridge University Press, 2010.

Taliaferro, Charles, and Paul Copan, eds. *The Naturalness of Belief*. London: Lexington, 2019.

Taliaferro, Charles, and Jil Evans. *Is God Invisible? An Essay on Religion and Aesthetics*. Cambridge: Cambridge University Press, 2021.

Taliaferro, Charles, and Rachel Traughber. "The Atonement in Narnia." In *The Chronicles of Narnia and Philosophy*, edited by Gregory Bassham and Jerry Walls, 245–59. Chicago: Open Court, 2005.

Tolkien, J. R. R. *The Adventures of Tom Bombadil*. London: Allen & Unwin, 1973.

————. "On Fairy Stories." Online: https://coolcalvary.files.wordpress.com/2018/10/on-fairy-stories1.pdf (accessed March 31, 2022).

Underhill, Evelyn. *The Greyworld*. London: Heinemann, 1904.

Walls, Jerry. "Heaven and Hell." In *The Cambridge Companion to Christian Philosophical Theology*, edited by Charles Taliaferro and Chad Meister, 238–52. Cambridge: Cambridge University Press, 2010.

————. *Purgatory: The Logic of Total Transformation*. Oxford: Oxford University Press, 2011.

Williams, Charles. *Descent into Hell*. Reprint, Durham, NC: Lulu, 2012.

Werther, David, and Susan Werther, eds. *C. S. Lewis's List: The Top Ten Books That Influenced Him*. London: Bloomsbury, 2015.

"What C. S. Lewis Said about Susan's Fate in *The Last Battle*." Narniaweb. https://www.narniaweb.com/2021/08/what-c-s-lewis-said-about-susans-fate-in-the-last-battle/ (accessed March 31, 2022).

Printed in Dunstable, United Kingdom

70372561R00088